AF255497

THE HAUNTED TRAIL

By

John Lukegord

TABLE OF CONTENTS

CHAPTER 1

A small ten-year-old boy roamed a few miles past his home in the backwoods of Dublin, Ireland. The path he walked was narrow and surrounded by tall, green bushes. The backwoods of Dublin were referred to by locals as the "Dublin Woods." The Dublin Woods sat on legendary woodland nearby a river, a mountainside, and an insane asylum. The area was considered legendary because of a wicked curse that had plagued this area on Halloween night for the past two thousand years. Some locals were very cautious of this curse and refused to set foot in this area on Halloween night, while others refused to believe the rumors. They were completely unaware of the reality and danger of these horrific woods.

The area became cursed two thousand years ago during the bloody end of a horrific war between Ireland and Egypt that took place in the Dublin Woods. The Dublin Mountains were dangerous terrain, with steep cliffs and jagged rocks throughout. The asylum nearby was called the Dublin Mental Institution and was said to be haunted by this same curse.

The small boy who walked this path was oblivious to the existence of this awful curse that wreaked havoc in the Dublin Woods on Halloween night. This boy's name was Dylan McGilicutty. Dylan had blond hair, and he wore a green hat. He was an overly curious boy who happened to wander upon a farm and a garden and noticed a giant scarecrow seemingly protecting the garden. A few weeks back, Mr. McGilicutty noticed that some of his ripe corn had been harvested. He assumed that his neighbor, Mr. O'Sullivan, had been responsible for stealing his corn. He informed his son Dylan about this and warned him to stay off the O'Sullivan property: Mr. McGilicutty no longer trusted his neighbor. While Dylan usually listened to his father, this incident bothered him, and he wanted revenge. His anger led him to steal Mr. O'Sullivan's scarecrow that overlooked his farm, and he did so on Halloween night of 1892, at 5:33 p.m.

Dylan, however, was unfamiliar with the scarecrow's sinister history. The scarecrow was a symbol of worship to a crazy, inbred farmer like Patrick O'Sullivan. This particular scarecrow was the sacred symbol of the garden, which led to a haunted trail. It was the heart and evil soul of the garden. Other scarecrows were scattered about the garden, but none was as big and important to O'Sullivan.

Patrick had handcrafted the scarecrow. He took pride in stuffing it with hay and stitching it together with his two filthy hands. He had constructed his scarecrow on Halloween of 1890. He believed the scarecrow was sacred, although it was just a silly-looking thing stuffed with hay. A few of the locals believed in what O'Sullivan preached about his sacred scarecrow. On the other hand, some of the locals thought he was out of touch with reality. The scarecrow did, however, serve as an efficient prop that kept most of the crows away. An abundance of crows could potentially damage or ruin edible crops. O'Sullivan grew and harvested his crops so the evil that lay within that wicked area could have food.

Along Dylan's route, he noticed a No Trespassing sign that he chose to ignore. Not far into the garden stood the sacred scarecrow, proudly perched on a wooden post. To reach the scarecrow, Dylan had to run a few hundred yards across the field, ultimately exposing himself to O'Sullivan's watchful eye. He had to be quick and quiet as he passed O'Sullivan's small shack.

Patrick was a former mental patient who had violent tendencies toward all living creatures. On September 7, 1870, a zookeeper had caught O'Sullivan abusing a helpless sheep. People who witnessed this were very unfortunate. Patrick had been warned by the zookeeper not to show his face at the Dublin Zoo ever again, but he hadn't listened to the zookeeper's warning. Again, he showed up at the zoo and abused animals. For the second time in a week, the public witnessed O'Sullivan's rage.

The zookeeper had attempted to rescue a sheep from O'Sullivan's clutches. O'Sullivan had drawn a metal trowel, which he had sharpened with a rock, from the back pocket of his dirty overalls and swiped its edge across the zookeeper's throat, fatally cutting his jugular. O'Sullivan was immediately apprehended by a group of citizens and turned over to the authorities.

Patrick O'Sullivan was sentenced to the Dublin Mental Institution for twenty years. He was released from the Dublin Mental Institution on September 7, 1890. He was now forty-five years old. He had cultivated the evil garden for a little over two years. All the lights were off in the shack as Patrick rested his body from a long day in the fields. He got up at the crack of dawn daily to worship the scarecrow before his workday. He also did the same thing at the end of the day. He had a strong affinity for worship, and not a day went by that he did not fulfill this ritual.

He spent most of his days angrily shooting his rifle at crows attempting to fly near his sacred scarecrow. As Dylan approached the scarecrow, Patrick was lying down on a hammock and just beginning to rest his eyes. Out of the corner of his eye and through a dust-stained window, Patrick noticed Dylan crawling up the wooden post that held his sacred idol. He knew his rifle was out of bullets. Fearing it would take too long to load his gun, Patrick grabbed his pitchfork and charged out the door. His protective nature over the garden and scarecrow enabled him to move more quickly than Dylan anticipated.

Dylan managed to knock the scarecrow off its post, but he was unable to lift the heavy idol. He noticed O'Sullivan running toward him with a pitchfork, and decided to run to the McArthur property.

**

Unknown to Dylan were the tendencies of the McArthur family. Scott McArthur, the head of the household, was a stern husband and father who saw himself as the sworn protector of the Dublin Woods. Scott had met his wife, Wendy, at a downtown pub on March 17, 1878.

Flanagan's Pub had been crowded on that St. Patrick's Day. Corned beef and boiled potatoes were served as complimentary platters. About a hundred Dublin locals had been eating and drinking in the small pub before noon. Alcoholics stumbled about in the pub, having a grand old time. A few altercations had occurred in the pub earlier that day, but the disgruntled drunks responsible for the violence had been escorted out. They were banned from the pub for the remainder of the St. Patrick's Day festivities.

Scott and Wendy had been dancing all day to the Irish music. A few men had been playing the bagpipes to liven up the spirit in the bar. When Scott first laid eyes on Wendy, he walked up to her and offered her a dance and a drink. She had given in to his politeness and couldn't resist his charm. He had been a perfect gentleman to her the whole day. They danced in the bar, lost in each other's eyes, until the final song of the evening. Scott and Wendy got married on St. Patrick's Day, 1879, exactly one year after they met. They got married in a small chapel and celebrated at Flanagan's afterward, then moved into a small cottage a mile away from Flanagan's. A month after their marriage, Scott and Wendy quit drinking and decided to leave their good old days at Flanagan's Pub behind them. They were even discussing having children.

Scott fished and farmed for his daily earnings, and he built houses. He was a man of many trades who kept himself occupied. He worked very hard to support himself and his wife. His experience and hard work eventually increased his earnings. He was smart with his money. He used his coin to pay for food and shelter. He saved everything he could for the opportunity for a better life. Scott and Wendy had dreams of living in a secluded area and raising two children. They knew their small cottage wasn't large enough to raise a family in, and the time had come for the McArthurs to leave their small cottage behind and pursue their dreams.

The McArthurs' dreams eventually came true, but so did their nightmares. Mary McArthur was eight years old and petrified of her strict father. Rarely did she disobey her short-tempered father. She knew forbidden behavior would result in punishment. She had been slapped around and beaten by her father last month for accidentally knocking over a fruit basket at three in the morning. She'd woken her father up in the middle of the night, and he became enraged over the fruit basket accident. "What the hell are you doing up past your bedtime?" he shouted at her, before giving her a few hard slaps to the face and shoving her to the ground. She lay on the kitchen floor and cried. "That's what you get for knocking over the damn basket. It's too late for you to be eating fruit. Get up right now and get your ass in that bedroom!"

She got up quickly and ran back into her bedroom. She had minor injuries from the incident, but the mental abuse of the situation affected her more than the beating. As early October approached, she noticed her father getting stricter by the day. Mary never snuck out of bed late at night to grab fruit after that one time. She peered out her bedroom window on sleepless nights during the month of October and noticed her father walking past their property, deep into the forest. She had no idea why.

The McArthur's son was a ten-year-old, disobedient little brat named Billy. Billy's disobedience resulted in beatings from his father. Scott was no longer the mentally stable person he once was—he had violent tendencies toward his family and utterly dominated their lives.

A violent altercation with a cursed mummy had turned Scott permanently insane. The mummy and its followers came from Egypt in a giant war boat two thousand years ago and invaded Ireland. The mummy and its followers had invaded in search of a rare four-leaf clover with magic healing powers that was located in Ireland. The mummy carried the very curse of the Dublin Woods in its evil heart and was killed in the Irish-Egyptian war two thousand years ago. The mummy lay in a burial ground in the Dublin Woods, and its cursed soul would come alive on Halloween night.

Scott had accidentally stepped on the mummy's grave, and it had risen from the grave and attacked him. On Halloween night of 1879, Scott McArthur had been searching the Dublin Woods to claim new property. He had heard a rumor from a crazy drunk at Flanagan's that the Dublin Woods was a death trap on Halloween night, but he was unsure if the drunk at Flanagan's was telling the truth, or just speaking nonsense. Scott learned that a curse had been placed on the Dublin Woods.

That night, he stepped on a cursed gravestone, and the mummy had suddenly risen from the grave and attacked him. The mummy attack happened very quickly and without any warning. Scott claimed that the mummy wore thick, white strips of cloth all along its body. He also claimed that the mummy's face had distorted flesh with a hideous, bloodshot, purple eye on the top of its skull. The mummy had managed to grab Scott's face and cause a devastating injury. Scott panicked and tried to detach this frightening creature from his face. He saw glimpses of the creature as it strangled him.

Scott thought that the demonic mummy was going to kill him.

After struggling for nearly a minute, Scott was able to detach the mummy from his face. The mummy suddenly vanished into thin air. Scott's face was bleeding, and his neck turned a red color due to loss of oxygen. He yelled out in fear and covered up his bloody face. No one heard Scott's fearful yelling. The mummy managed to rip some of the skin from Scott's face near his right cheek. The mummy could have easily killed Scott McArthur if it wanted to. What the mummy wanted instead was revenge. Revenge for what his ancestor, Connor McArthur did to it two thousand years ago in the war. Connor McArthur had fired a flaming arrow at the mummy's chest in the war and the mummy's heart had been damaged. Two blue aliens had repaired the mummy's heart after it had been struck by the flaming arrow. The mummy had a vivid memory of this past occurrence. The mummy chose to poison Scott's mind with an evil curse and make him its slave. After this terrible incident occurred, Scott was never the same. Scott experienced horrible flashbacks from the relentless mummy altercation. He couldn't get the horrible images from the mummy attack out of his mind, and this ultimately led to his insanity.

Immediately after the frightening incident, Scott fled the Dublin Woods and miraculously escaped from the cursed mummy. Scott was left with a disfigured face, along with serious mental scarring. Even though Wendy thought that the mummy was a brief hallucination in Scott's mind, he had scars on his face to prove that an altercation had happened. Wendy's marriage then became hostile. From then on, she took verbal and physical abuse from her husband. She was coerced by her husband into believing she was a pitiful human being. He turned hostile toward his wife because of the overwhelming mental stress caused by the mummy attack.

Scott voluntarily admitted himself into the Dublin Mental Institution because he realized his anger and his fears frightened his wife. While serving his time in the institution, he befriended the Killington brothers. McArthur and the Killington brothers met in the dining hall of the facility and they became friends. His two new friends, the Infamous Killington Brothers, were identical twins who had served a thirty-year sentence in the Dublin Mental Institution for multiple homicides.

On Halloween of 1880, they were allowed back into society. Because Scott McArthur was a voluntary patient at the facility, he could request permission to leave whenever he wanted. He planned his own release date from the institution on the same day the Killington brothers were let out.

The Killington brothers were well-connected with evil people in Dublin. The two brothers had associated themselves with other lunatics in the Dublin area before they were sent away for murder charges. They had befriended many other mentally ill individuals during their long sentence at the Dublin Mental Institution. Within a week of their release, the Killington brothers reconnected with the lunatics they had associated with years ago. McArthur showed these lunatics his deformed face and informed them that a cursed mummy was the cause. He told his evil friends that the mummy was a supernatural creature from somewhere way beyond this world.

McArthur convinced these men that this supernatural creature existed and that the Dublin Woods were cursed.

The curse of the asylum never left this small group of men. When these men were released back into society, they assisted McArthur with his sinister plans and became members of his evil cult. McArthur did not regain his grasp on reality because of his time in the mental hospital. He and his crew began constructing his house and command post on November 8, 1880. Twenty men participated in the operation and finished the construction on McArthur's land on December 31, 1880.

The command post was built on McArthur's property line for strict security purposes. The men built the fortress out of stone pillars. It was circular, about fifty feet high, and had stone staircases spiraling from top to bottom. A turret rose from the center of McArthur's personal fortress. McArthur stood guard on his command post and monitored his property line for any potential intruders.

He stood guard at his post most of the time. He rigged a light atop his fortress so he could spot suspicious activity near his property line at night. When the skies were dark, McArthur had a difficult time seeing through the lens of his turret. The mist from the air would occasionally fog up the lens. The command post was located a hundred feet away from the McArthurs' house.

Scott and his family moved into their new home on New Year's Day, 1881. Their wooden house had four small rooms plus a small kitchen. Ten feet outside the house stood a shack with a large bucket inside. The family used the large bucket inside of their shack to collect their urine and feces. There was a stack of medical paper stored on a wooden shelf in the shack. And on the floor, there was another very small bucket, half-full of water, right next to the large bucket. This small bucket of water was used for sanitation purposes.

The McArthurs also had another small bucket that they used to store their water supply. Wendy walked to the riverbed and filled up the little bucket with water a few times a day. The Dublin River was their source of water for cooking, sanitation, and hydration, and was located about a mile south of the McArthur property line.

Soon after the McArthurs moved into their property, Scott's followers constructed small shacks in the Dublin Woods and resided behind his land. McArthur's men monitored the terrain behind his property line for trespassers. McArthur needed the assistance of these deranged men in his evil quest to protect the Dublin Woods.

They set up kill stations near their shacks and spread themselves throughout a three-mile perimeter in the cursed woods. They constructed a cannon near the southern tip of the Dublin River. Killing devices such as a guillotine, an electric chair, a noose, a chef station operated by a cannibal, and a pendulum were all located in the dangerous terrain behind the haunted cemetery of the Dublin Mental Institution. Evil men lived in dwellings near these kill stations.

These men followed McArthur's commands and executed anyone who dared trespass on Halloween night. They referred to Scott McArthur as the "Protector of the Dublin Woods." McArthur felt he had a strict duty to protect his property line and made sure that nobody entered or exited the Dublin Woods on Halloween night.

**

While Dylan was escaping from his encounter with O'Sullivan by running toward the McArthur property, the McArthurs were having a dispute of their own. Little Billy McArthur, Scott's son, was constantly told not to play in the yard while his father was at his command post. Scott felt it was extremely important to protect the integrity of the woods, and for that reason, his son was not allowed to have any fun or to live like a normal ten-year-old kid. Scott constantly told Billy, "Stay out of the fucking yard while I'm working."

Today was no different. Scott had a lot of trouble controlling his anger since the dreadful night the mummy had attacked him. He'd been living with this mental sickness for thirteen years. This time, however, Billy managed to escape from the confines of the McArthur property. Earlier that evening, Scott and Wendy had had a fight—Scott had given her a savage beating after she had accidentally overcooked the chicken dinner.

Wendy had been icing down her swollen eye in the kitchen as the children of this dysfunctional family were having a dispute of their own in their bedroom. Billy's younger sister Mary was pleading, "If the haunted trail doesn't kill you, Billy, Dad will!"

"Fuck this," said Billy. "I'm getting out of this stupid family, and you should come with me! You saw the beating Dad gave Mom for ruining the chicken. It's not safe here. I'm leaving and never coming back." Although Mary refused to go, Billy decided to leave anyway.

Billy approached his bedroom window, forcefully kicked it, and escaped the confines of the property. Scott heard the crash of the window breaking, and as he looked over toward the noise, he saw Billy running away. Scott became infuriated when he saw his son defying him. He decided to leave his post to chase after his nuisance of a son. "Damn it, that fucking kid," Scott said as he grabbed his spiked bat and headed down the fortress's stone spiral staircase.

At that moment, Dylan came running onto the McArthurs' property. On a normal day, Dylan would have been shot on sight, but Scott was no longer at his post. Upon entering the property, the crazed farmer O'Sullivan cautioned loudly, "Protector of the Dublin Woods, intruder alert! I need backup!"

But there was no one to hear the call. The chase for Dylan continued into unknown Dublin territory. Dylan had never ventured this far from his house and this far into the woods. He was unaware of the fact that throughout history many people had been murdered in these cursed woods. The level of fear racing through his body led him to run faster and jump higher than he thought possible.

As night fell, Dylan maneuvered through the McArthur property and into the deep forest. Dylan became even more frightened when he heard the sounds of wolves howling in the night. The paths he ran down were narrow, steep, and dark. He tripped on a jagged rock and fell into a set of thorn bushes. He got minor cuts on his hands and face after falling into the bushes. The adrenaline flowing through his body caused him to ignore the pain from the fall. Dylan quickly got up and continued running away, trying desperately to escape from this deranged farmer.

O'Sullivan was gaining on him and yelling profanities as he chased Dylan with his pitchfork drawn. "I'm gonna get ya, you little fuckin' hooligan!" shouted O'Sullivan. O'Sullivan tripped on the same jagged rock as Dylan dropped his pitchfork, and fell into the thorn bushes. He got minor cuts on his hands and face. O'Sullivan angrily shouted "Damn it," grabbed his pitchfork, and immediately got up and continued his foot pursuit of Dylan. The haunted trail ran directly behind McArthur's land, and Dylan had no choice but to enter this forbidden zone.

**

Just up the path lay the shack of Matthew Killington. Killington had been responsible for the Halloween Massacre of 1842. With the help of his twin brother, Martin, they had managed to behead six innocent children that night. The Killington brothers had decapitated the children in a field near the Dublin Woods. Shortly after the murders, the authorities had been made aware of the situation and formed a manhunt in an attempt to capture the people responsible for the crime.

The Killington brothers had attempted to bury all six children in the Dublin Woods to cover up their murders. They had managed to bury three children in the woods near the field. Halfway through the operation, the Killington brothers panicked and attempted to flee because the police had spotted them in the field. Their attempt to bury the bodies took the time they couldn't spare, and it ultimately compromised their own escape route. They were eventually caught by the authorities that night and confined to a jail cell in downtown Dublin. Eight years later, on Halloween of 1850, they were transferred to the Dublin Mental Institution.

This Halloween night happened to be the fifty-year anniversary of the massacre, and the Killington brothers had blood on their minds. Matthew was in luck this evening as he and little Dylan were on a crash course for one another. As Dylan approached, Killington heard somebody coming and hid behind a bush to see what was transpiring. Although it was dark, Killington managed to tackle this ten-year-old boy as he ran by the bush. Dylan had no chance, even though Killington was sixty-five years old and of small stature.

As the inbred O'Sullivan caught up to Dylan, he realized the boy had been captured and let out a sigh of relief. He and Killington were both bloodthirsty, and they had their prey. He shouted at Dylan, "You tampered with my scarecrow, and now you'll pay the price!"

His first thought was to stick him with the pitchfork, but then Killington pointed out his homemade guillotine. The guillotine had been handcrafted by Matthew Killington, with pieces of wood nailed together and used on Halloween night to kill innocent trespassers. A sharp guillotine blade was connected between two pieces of wood and attached atop the killing device. Once a victim was strapped to this killing device and the blade was detached, it quickly dropped between the pieces of wood and cut off any human flesh in its path. This contraption excited O'Sullivan very much. He grinned from ear to ear, and said, "Let's chop this little bastard's head off!"

Dylan realized that his curiosity had caught up with him for the last time and he was in real trouble now. He pleaded with the men, "Please don't kill me! I'm only a kid. I haven't done anything wrong. I'm sorry about your scarecrow, and I promise I'll make it up to you if you let me live. I didn't even take the scarecrow, so why do you want to kill me?"

"The scarecrow is forbidden," O'Sullivan hastily answered, "and now you'll pay for what you've done! It fell off its post; it no longer hangs proudly! I spent countless hours handcrafting my sacred scarecrow, and you've damaged it!" O'Sullivan said to Killington, "We're wasting time! Let's drag him over to the guillotine!"

He and Killington dragged Dylan to the guillotine and prepared it for use. Tears began forming in the young boy's eyes as he realized his fate. He began to think about the ten short years that he had roamed this godforsaken corner of Ireland. As O'Sullivan forced the four edges of the pitchfork into Dylan's back, it was clear that Dylan was terrified.

He was even more terrified as he laid eyes on the guillotine. As the men placed Dylan's neck on the guillotine, face down, one last bead of sweat ran down the young boy's face. They strapped Dylan down by his hands as Killington readied his death machine. O'Sullivan's eyes lit up as he continued to poke Dylan in the back aggressively. As Dylan took a final breath, Killington detached the rope and the guillotine blade dropped. The razor-sharp guillotine blade sliced brutally through Dylan's little neck, and his head fell into a wooden bucket under the guillotine.

O'Sullivan and Killington shook hands. As they parted ways, O'Sullivan said, "Nice doing business with you. I must return to the farm and fix my broken scarecrow."

"Okay," said Killington, "I have to bury this little bastard anyways, so I'll see you soon."

As Dylan was being beheaded, McArthur and his son were having a dispute of their own. When Scott eventually caught up to Billy, he said, "Look at me, you disobedient son of a bitch! The woods are cursed, and now you are too. Now I must kill you before the curse of the mummy does." He swung his spiked bat and struck Billy in the head.

Even after Billy was dead, McArthur continued to strike his son with the bat. Billy was now bloodied from head to torso, and McArthur finally stopped to realize what he had done. Scott walked about a mile to his property as wolves began to devour the corpse of his slain son.

Ten minutes later, Scott had made it home. He put his spiked bat down on the ground next to the front door of the house. He took a nervous deep breath and walked into his house. He walked into his living room. Wendy looked at him. She had a worried look on her face.

"Did you find our son?" she asked.

"No. I didn't. He's still missing."

Scott hugged his wife, looked into her crushed eyes, and said, "If he doesn't return home tonight, I'll search the woods in the morning." They held each other tightly and cried. A brief moment had passed. After Scott had just finished lying to his wife he walked outside, grabbed his spiked bat, and returned to his command post. Wendy sat on her couch in the living room as she worried about the whereabouts of her son.

**

Patrick O'Sullivan had just arrived back at his garden. He walked over to his scarecrow. He was extremely disgruntled because his scarecrow had been tampered with. He put his pitchfork down on the ground next to the scarecrow. He picked up his scarecrow, wiped the dirt off it, and said, "That little hooligan tampered with my damn scarecrow. I fuckin' hate kids." Patrick took a look at his scarecrow to inspect the damage. He looked at the scarecrow for a few seconds, then he was distracted when he saw a man storming toward his garden in a fit of rage. This man was Roger McGilicutty. He was Dylan McGilicutty's father. Patrick hung his scarecrow up on the wooden post. He turned his attention toward Roger. Roger said, "Hey, asshole, where the fuck is my son?"

"Your little hooligan son tampered with my fuckin' scarecrow, so I chased him down with my pitchfork. Keep off my property!"

"Go fuck yourself, you inbred piece of shit!"

Roger ran right up to Patrick O'Sullivan and socked him in the face with a right hook. O'Sullivan fell backward a few feet, then dropped to the ground. He was dazed for a second, then he snapped out of it. Blood was dripping from his mouth. He spit out blood and a broken tooth. A second later, he looked over and saw his pitchfork right next to him. He picked the pitchfork up and struck Roger in the stomach with it just as Roger was about to attack him again. Roger grunted in pain; then he instantly died. "Fuck you and your hooligan son!" shouted O'Sullivan. O'Sullivan took the pitchfork out of his enemies' stomach and wiped the pitchfork on the ground to get the blood off. He put his pitchfork down. He dragged Roger a mile away to near the Dublin Mountain. Then he walked back to his property. Vicious wolves devoured Roger's corpse. O'Sullivan went back over to his scarecrow to inspect it for damage.

CHAPTER 2

While these murderous scenes were unfolding, three brothers were floating down the southern loop of the Dublin River on a fishing trip. The Patrican brothers were very close-knit and always had one another's backs. Today would be no different. Normally these men liked to fish on the public side of the Dublin River. Their mother always told them not to go past a certain landmark on the river because of the evil that lurked beyond, but they never truly understood the significance of this advice until today.

As the drunken brothers approached a no-trespassing sign, they all looked at each other and said, "Fuck it. Let's do this."

As they pushed on farther than they ever had, they heard a kind voice saying, "Turn back now. Danger is ahead. Just a friendly warning." They decided to shrug off the warning and continue. The friendly warning came from the ghost of General Butch McPherson, who had been an Irish soldier in his past life nearly two thousand years ago. The ghost of General Butch McPherson only came out on Halloween night to fight for peace. No one had ever seen this friendly ghost in its two thousand years of existence.

Henry Patrican was thirty, and the oldest of the three brothers. He was a role model for his younger siblings. He'd had to step up and be the man of the house when their father had died in a horrific coal-mining accident. Their father was Brian Patrican.

The accident happened on April 12, 1877, which made things very difficult for the Patrican family. This shocking death had devastated his mother, Sandra. She did her best to raise her three sons after her husband passed away. She passed away from natural causes on August 9, 1889.

Henry's younger brother, Wayne, had been ten when his father died. He had had a difficult time dealing with the loss of his father. He had gone fishing with his father on the Dublin River the night before the accident. The memory of fishing with his father kept flowing through his mind during his father's funeral.

The youngest, Mick, had been two at the time of the father's death. He only vaguely remembered who his father was. Henry was a father figure to both his younger brothers, but especially to Mick.

The Patrican brothers were forever grateful for everything their parents had done for them. The Patricans were a poor family who barely made ends meet. The three kids grew up together and formed a strong brotherhood bond that could never be broken. They looked alike: all had dirty blonde hair and crewcuts, and they had similar builds. Wayne, the middle child, was now twenty-five years old. His hobbies were drinking and fishing, and he shared these hobbies with both of his brothers. At the age of seventeen, Mick Patrican was a small, rugged Irishman. Even Mick was unaware of the strength of this brotherhood bond.

The Patrican brothers had built their boat a few years back out of scrap wood, and they had taken it on many fishing trips. They kept their boat in very good condition, which was something their father ingrained in them from a young age. The Patrican brothers caught fish from the river and sold their catch to local merchants. Fishing was their greatest passion in life and their means of survival, but the Patrican brothers now took their fishing boat into the heart of the forbidden territory.

A short distance up the river, on the right side of the riverbed, Harry McFloyd was carving his name and tonight's date with a knife on the granite of his cannon. After he finished marking his cannon, he stood on it. McFloyd stood atop the cannon and peered down the riverbed for trespassing vessels. McFloyd had been a pyromaniac growing up, and he had served time in the Dublin Mental Institution's juvenile facility for setting a grade school ablaze on Halloween 1884. Harry was a dropout punk at the age of twelve when he committed this horrible act. He hated school and all the teachers, so he rebelled against them. With one accurate toss of a flaming bottle, Harry had taken out the Dublin grade school. Harry had listened to the voices in his head that told him to destroy the school, but he had been caught by the authorities as he tried to escape into the woods near the blazing schoolyard. He told the authorities about these evil voices in his head. The authorities sentenced McFloyd to the juvenile facility until he turned eighteen.

Just looking at this kid's smile was a nightmare. He had horrible-looking teeth and an evil smile. Harry had hideous acne all over his face and a blond mullet. He was released from the juvenile facility on April 1, 1890. He resided in a shack near the Dublin River. McFloyd was now twenty years old. He kept trespassers away from this territory of the Dublin Woods. He had constructed a small cannon alongside the riverbed as a defense mechanism aimed at trespassing vessels. McFloyd built his cannon out of granite and carefully carved it so that a small cannonball could blast out of it at nearly two hundred miles per hour. McFloyd only used his cannon on Halloween night. Green bushes surrounded the outer perimeter, hiding the cannon.

Harry had a loyal four-man crew of homeless, mentally ill people who worked under his command. These men were homeless because they were too stupid to construct a shack. Despite their inability to build a dwelling, they happened to be very good at capturing trespassers. Their hunting abilities were excellent, and that's why they were so valuable to McFloyd. They monitored the riverbed for trespassers.

As the Patrican brothers continued to sail down the river, Harry heard them and spotted the boat from a short distance away. Harry signaled to his crew roaming the territory nearby that trespassers were approaching. This meant that the four other guards under McFloyd's command were fully aware that a boat was headed toward their section of the river. As the Patrican brothers drifted further down the river, Harry prepared to blast his cannonball. Harry McFloyd was a sneaky little punk, and he took ultimate pride in blindsided cannonball attacks.

Harry quietly waited for the Patrican brothers to drift into his range. As the boat sailed into Harry's sights, the loud sound of a blasting cannonball echoed throughout the area. The boat took a serious blow from the cannonball. Heavily damaged, the boat drifted toward its port side and was about to sink.

Henry yelled to his younger brothers, "We're under attack! Abandon ship!"

Seconds later, his mouth filled with water as he and his brothers sank into the river.

McFloyd's security force jumped into the river. Henry and Wayne were immediately captured. Henry and Wayne could not swim away quickly enough to escape. The sinking boat caused a powerful current in which Henry and Wayne were both caught. As for Mick, he remained underwater and was temporarily unspotted. The four guards wasted no time dragging Wayne and Henry out of the river.

Harry ran into his shack and grabbed a few small sets of rope. The four guards beat up the two oldest Patrican brothers. Henry and Wayne were outnumbered and unable to escape or defend themselves. Meanwhile, Mick was trying to elude these men and escape to a safe distance. Mick held his breath for nearly two minutes until he slowly raised his head above water. He slowly and silently took a couple of desperate breaths. He feared that his older brothers had both been captured.

More guards swarmed the terrain, and there was nothing he could do to save his brothers. Henry and Wayne were being badly beaten by the forest-dwelling lunatics. In a matter of minutes, the Patrican brothers were outnumbered twelve to three. Seven other lunatics who were roaming the woods nearby had heard the cannon and ran over toward the river to assist with the manhunt.

McFloyd ran over toward his evil companions and shouted, "They're guilty of trespassing on our forbidden turf, and they both must be executed. Tie these two up with my ropes immediately! As for the third trespasser on the ship, capture him and tie him up as well!"

McFloyd's crewmembers grabbed some loose rope and began to tie up Henry and Wayne. A few of the guards roamed the terrain nearby in search of the third brother. Mick quietly submerged again to avoid being spotted. He slowly came up for air and quietly swam toward land. He crawled out of the riverbed. The guards searched different areas nearby in their attempt to capture him. Mick was a few hundred feet away from his brothers, and he could see them both being tortured and dragged against their will. Mick wished he could heroically rescue his older brothers, but he couldn't help them because he was in a desperate attempt to save himself.

Henry was now being dragged in the direction of the electric chair. The electric chair was located a few hundred yards away from the cannon. It had electrical wiring attached all around it, and a metal headset connected to the wiring. The electric chair had metal straps connected to its arms and legs.

Miles O'Neill, the designer and operator of the electric chair, waited for him. Miles had yet to kill anyone with this death machine, but he stood next to it and grinned with a sinister smile as his first victim was being dragged toward him. Miles was found guilty of the murder of a coworker back on April 12, 1877. He had been a supervisor in the coal-mining fields, and he had a violent episode against a lazy new employee who had made a critical mistake. Miles murdered the man, Gerald Gilligan, while he was on the job.

Gerald had been responsible for securing the entry to a new mine that had just been dug out and was not yet fully secured. As the diggers had been attempting to exit the mine, the entryway collapsed on them, leaving them stuck in a hole thirty feet down. Miles had seen this collapse. In the moment of passion, Miles became enraged and pushed Gerald off the edge into the hole. In all, twelve people died, but the remaining miners told the authorities the story about Gilligan's death. Brian Patrican was one of the miners trapped.

Miles served fifteen years in the Dublin Mental Institution and had been released just over six months ago. Miles was fifty-two years old. He had red hair and a scruffy beard and lived in a small shack right next to his electric chair. The chair worked perfectly now after a few initial design flaws. Miles couldn't wait to use his death chair on the trespasser he saw captured in the distance.

Henry was being dragged closer and closer to Miles. "Hurry up, you bumbling idiots, and put him in the fucking chair!" Miles shouted to the guards.

Henry was injured and unable to escape or defend himself against the guards. "Strap him into the chair!" Miles said. The guards shoved Henry into the electric chair. The guards punched him in the face a few times after they strapped him in. Miles secured the metal headgear on Henry's skull.

Miles pointed at his victim and shouted, "You're my first victim. You shall be executed on this Halloween night for the crime of trespassing on these sacred grounds. This is the end of your time!"

He engaged the power function of the chair. After about a minute, the chair started to heat up. Henry could feel the intensity of the electric energy sizzling his skull, affecting every part of his body. He began to foam at the mouth. Henry Patrican's eyes were filled with overwhelming fear as he knew he was about to die. Over several seconds, the electric jolt of energy frying Henry Patrican's body became much more harmful. As his flesh started to burn, smoke rose into the dark air. Miles and the mentally disturbed guards watched from nearby. They could smell the burning flesh in the autumn air. Henry saw a bright green ghost glow right in front of his eyes. Henry thought that he was hallucinating. The ghost spoke to him and said, "Don't be afraid, Henry. I'm here to help you. I'm the ghost of General Butch McPherson. Your family has a special gift. The fate of all that is good in Dublin rests in your family's hands. Good luck, and be careful." Then the ghost vanished right before Henry's eyes. This was the end for the eldest brother, Henry Patrican.

Mick was still a few hundred feet away, and he knew the fate of his brothers was not good. Mick was petrified of these evil men.

Tears began to pour from Mick's eyes. Wayne Patrican was being dragged against his will toward the section of the woods belonging to Douglas O'Connor.

Douglas O'Connor was a former mental patient at the Dublin Mental Institution's juvenile facility. Douglas and his best friend, Ronald O'Leary, had been found guilty of beating and lynching a woman on Halloween night of 1885 in a secluded section of the Dublin Woods nearby the mountainside. They had been convinced this woman was a witch, and, based on their perception, this act had seemed like no big deal to them. Douglas and Ronald were two evil young kids who were just looking for an excuse to kill an innocent woman on Halloween night. Douglas and Ronald had roamed this area and claimed it as their turf. The two young men became enraged when they saw that a crazy woman was trespassing on their territory.

The woman's name was Rosemary McCloud. She had been practicing witchcraft in the woods around a fire, holding a wand and chanting gibberish when the boys ambushed her. She never saw them coming, and she had no chance to defend herself. Rosemary screamed for help, but nobody was nearby to hear her desperate cries. She was hanged on a rope swing used by local kids. Her dead body rested there in the dark woods, attached by the neck to the noose. Douglas and Ronald gloated over their kill for a few minutes, then left the area.

Immediately after this attack, Douglas and Ronald went to the authorities to explain what they had done. They said they had killed a dangerous witch in the woods and that they had done society a huge favor. Upon hearing this, the local authorities investigated this violent incident and arrested the two boys on murder charges. The authorities dismantled the rope swing and kept it for evidence. The boys had been convinced that what they did was justified and saw no reason for their arrest.

Both these punks were only thirteen years old when they committed this brutal crime. They both pleaded insanity and were sentenced to serve time in the juvenile facility. Douglas and Ronald were confined until they turned eighteen.

The juvenile facility, built right next to the Dublin Mental Institution, was a jail for mentally defective minors. It was fully constructed in the summer of 1880 and became fully functional as an institution on August 22, 1880. The warden of the Dublin Mental Institution had been left a vast fortune in his family will, giving him the resources to construct the juvenile facility. The building was constructed with one hundred cells to contain juvenile delinquents. Each cell had a bathroom, and the bathrooms were equipped with a toilet and a faucet. There was a shower room in the facility that was equipped with one hundred showers. This institution was completely full of one hundred troubled youths from the ages of ten to seventeen. No mental patient over the age of seventeen was allowed to serve time in the juvenile facility. Once a mental patient turned eighteen, he was either transferred to the Dublin Mental Institution or released back into society.

Ronald had been brutally killed in the juvenile facility on his first day, and beaten to death by an angry gang because he had a tendency to run his mouth. Ronald had claimed that he was the toughest kid in the institution, but he was proven wrong when the angry lunatics ganged up on him in the showers and beat him to death.

Douglas had told Ronald that he would stick up for him if anything dangerous went down, but Douglas had stood back and nervously watched as the gang beat his best friend to death. Somehow he had managed to survive in the dangerous facility. After serving just less than five years, Douglas had been released. O'Connor and McFloyd had become very close friends while they served time together in the dangerous institution. Coincidentally, they both had their parole hearing on the same day. These two mental defectives had turned eighteen on the same day, April 1, 1890. On that day, they had been allowed back into society. When they got out, they had become part of McArthur's cult. The cult members felt that these two troublemakers were perfect—young, evil blood to keep the future of the clan going strong.

For the last two years, Douglas had been residing in a small shack in the Dublin Woods. He had a tree with a hanging noose near his shack. O'Connor was a tall man, standing six feet eight inches. He could reach the end of his noose with no problem while standing on the ground. Douglas's kill station was located a few hundred feet away from the shack housing Miles O'Neill.

**

Douglas looked over to see the frantic kicking and screaming of a new victim. Wayne Patrican was being dragged over in the direction of Douglas and the noose. Douglas said, "Dublin guards, bring this forbidden trespasser over to me immediately! I want him to suffer on Halloween just like that bitch Rosemary McCloud!"

The guards forced Wayne over to the noose. Douglas ordered Wayne to stand on the stool beneath the rope, but he couldn't even stand up. The guards held him up on his feet because he was unable to keep his balance as they aggressively forced him onto the stool. Douglas walked over to Wayne and placed the noose around his neck. Wayne had a helpless look on his face. He had been badly beaten and was unable to escape or fight back. His eyes were so swollen he could barely see, and his lips were so swollen he was unable to beg for his life or say his last words.

Douglas pointed at Wayne and shouted, "You will be lynched for your forbidden trespass!" After that, Douglas kicked the stool from under Wayne Patrican's legs. Wayne Patrican was hanged, and his feet kicked in the air. Wayne saw a bright green ghost glow right before his eyes. It was the ghost of General Butch McPherson. Wayne thought that he was hallucinating. The ghost of General Butch McPherson said to him, "I lost a magical clover in a cave two thousand years ago during a war. You must find the clover in order to save Ireland." Then the ghost vanished right before his eyes. This was the end for Wayne Patrican. The mental guards cheered because of another successful Halloween execution. Shortly after the executions, the Patrican brothers' bodies were moved by the guards and dumped into the Dublin River.

The guards roamed further into the terrain to search for Mick Patrican. Mick remained silent as one of the guards headed in his direction. Mick grabbed a few slabs of mud and began to cover his face and any exposed skin, camouflaging himself in the dark night, making it much harder for the guards to spot him. Mick got on his hands and knees and quietly maneuvered around a tree to avoid being spotted. He hid behind the tree until the guard moved on to search a different section of the Dublin trails.

Patrican wanted to leave this cursed section of Dublin because he knew his life was in danger, but he was way too stubborn to leave just yet. Patrican felt he must avenge the deaths of his two older brothers. He decided to move to a more secluded area. When the guards fanned out to different regions of the trail to widen their search, he would strike. Mick knew that fighting back against these insane killers was even more dangerous than trying to escape from them. Mick wasn't backing down, though. He planned the murders of the electric chair operator and the man with the noose. Mick ran further into the woods. But the particular section along which Patrican trespassed was where the curse of the Dublin Woods originated.

As Mick moved along, he trespassed over a small patch of grass with a broken tombstone in the middle of it. Mick had accidentally stepped on the ancient burial ground of the cursed mummy. The mummy angrily rose from its grave and attacked him. When the mummy grabbed his left arm, Mick jumped back in terror, but he managed to shrug off the grip and strike the mummy in its chest with a powerful right-handed punch. This blow to the chest had stunned the mummy's heart. The mummy groaned in pain as it held its chest with its left hand, then collapsed. The mummy lay there, motionless. The mummy was unconscious. Seconds later, the mummy suddenly transformed itself into a naked blue alien and then it vanished into thin air. Patrican screamed and then fled the area of the cursed burial ground immediately after he saw the mummy turn into a frightening blue alien and fade away into thin air. The only wound on Patrican's body was a red handprint on his left arm.

Mick Patrican had successfully defended himself against the mummy. The legend of the mummy goes back two thousand years. For two thousand years, many Irishmen believed that no man could defend himself against the mummy and the terrible curses it possessed. Patrican was too determined and strong-minded to suffer from this horrific curse. It was a miracle that the curse of the mummy didn't affect him.

The mental guards roamed, searching the Dublin trails with lanterns in pursuit of the last surviving Patrican brother. They suspected Patrican to be near the mummy's grave. The guards knew not to disturb the area near the mummy's grave because of the fearful curse. One of the guards had a vicious dog that Patrican could hear growling from a distance.

In a short time, the twelve guards were completely confused. Mick made it far away from the angry mob and took cover in a small ditch. The twelve Dublin guards diverted their manpower to a different region of the trail. As Patrican emerged from the ditch, he spotted an unguarded path that led back in the direction where both of his older brothers had been executed. Patrican's revenge was only a few hundred feet away.

Patrican tiptoed, quietly moving closer and closer to the electric chair. He planned heavy revenge on Miles O'Neill. Patrican drew out his small fishing knife. He held his weapon tightly in his right hand as he snuck behind Miles's shack. As Miles stood next to his post, he heard a noise from behind his shed. Miles grabbed his lantern and, as he rounded the corner, held out his lantern for better night vision. Patrican snuck up on Miles and brutally stabbed him in the throat. Miles dropped to the ground in agony. As Miles lay there dazed and bleeding, Patrican picked him up and said, "You took away my brother. It's time for you to pay for your sins."

He threw Miles onto the electric chair and strapped him in. He strapped the metal headgear over Miles's skull and threw the lever. It took about ten seconds for the system to fully heat up. The electric chair was still very hot from its previous use. Miles started to feel the horrible sensation of his flesh burning. He screamed as he felt his skull sizzling. After a minute of torture, Miles was fried to death. Mick Patrican was unaware that the man he killed in the electric chair was formerly his father's foreman. Douglas heard Miles's shrieks, so he ran over to see what was going on.

Patrican hid behind Miles's shack. As O'Connor moved slightly closer, he noticed that his companion had just been fried to death. Douglas turned around and prepared to find a backup. Douglas had taken no more than two steps when Mick emerged from the darkness. Mick had his small fishing knife drawn, and he managed to slit Douglas's throat. Douglas O'Connor dropped to his bloody death.

After avenging the deaths of his two older brothers, Patrican fled the area and vanished quickly. When the guards spotted the smoke from a few hundred yards away, they headed toward the electric chair. When the guards all gathered, they discovered that two of their own had just been executed. After seeing these executions, Harry McFloyd rushed over to Scott McArthur's property to inform him of the murders. When Harry McFloyd walked onto McArthur's property, McArthur was standing guard at his command post with his turret aimed at McFloyd's head. When he realized it was Harry McFloyd, he stood down. McArthur looked down at him and waited for Harry to walk up the stairwell. When Harry walked up the stairwell, he said to McArthur, "Master McArthur, a goddamn trespasser took out O'Neill and O'Connor! I took out a small wooden boat with a cannonball shot. There were three men in the boat and the guards managed to take out two of them. The third trespasser came back for revenge and he took out two of our men. He bolted from the area after the killings. Your men are on the hunt for him as we speak."

"We can't let this fuck get away with this shit! We have to find this bastard and kill him! I'll join you on the search. Let's get moving."

"Yes, Master McArthur."

McArthur quickly grabbed his spiked bat. The two evil men headed out into the Dublin Woods to join the other lunatics in the search for the trespasser. Now the massive manhunt for Mick Patrican intensified.

CHAPTER 3

The annual Dublin Halloween Fair was going on about two miles outside of the no-trespassing section. A shady-looking clown of a man waited at his rigged carnival game. This man was a crooked carny as well as a burglar and a rapist. The clown wore a green suit and wig and went by the name of Herman McRandle. Herman painted his face with a white paste and dressed as a clown all the time. Herman McRandle was forty years old and was born on October 24, 1852. He didn't ever want people to see what he truly looked like.

Herman liked to travel with the fair and not stay in one town for too long. McRandle had been in and out of prisons since he was a hot-tempered youth. Herman had dressed up as a green clown for his grade school's Halloween costume party and murdered his schoolyard enemy; he had stabbed a kid named Thurman McDaniels to death with a metal fork in his school cafeteria. This incident had happened in a small town about thirty miles outside of Dublin.

Herman had serious emotional issues that riled up his blood. He had been disturbed ever since his father had passed away on his tenth birthday. He and his father were very close, and they both shared the name Herman McRandle. They both studied voodoo curses and read books on life after death. Herman's father taught him all sorts of shady tricks on how to hustle innocent people. His father also taught him how to break into houses and steal things such as jewelry, loose change, food, and anything of value.

On Herman's sixth birthday, he and his father took a few shots of rum, then they broke into a small bakery. They smashed the cash register and stole all the coins from it. The McRandles also stole fancy bakery equipment such as a stainless-steel bread maker, and a wooden rolling pin. The six-year-old drunken child was uncontrollably giggling in the bakery as he experienced his first break-in with his dishonest father. It was one of the McRandles' favorite father-son moments together. Herman's father was an expert at pulling off dishonest acts and not suffering the punishment for them, due to his sneakiness. Herman's father passed these dishonest traits onto his son. This was how Herman and his father lived to get by. Herman idolized his father and felt more lost than ever after his father's death.

Herman and Thurman were mortal enemies in the schoolyard. The kids treated these two children as outcasts and forced them to fight against each other because their names sounded so similar. They thought it was a fun thing to do during recess. Herman would come home from school with black eyes and bruises all over his body. He had outlasted his schoolyard enemy a few times; usually, however, Thurman would get the better of him in combat.

Herman spent his first night in the children's orphanage on October 30, 1862. Herman had a strange dream that night. His dead father revealed a deep family secret to him on the night before Halloween in 1862.

His dead father spoke to him in a dream and said, "Hey, Herman, it's me, Dad. I'm sorry that I died on your tenth birthday. I told you that life exists after death. Son, you have to kill Thurman McDaniels tomorrow. The kids at school will respect you more if you kill him on Halloween. Show everyone who the McRandles are. Thurman McDaniels' name belongs on a gravestone. Make your old man proud. I believe in you, Herman. Kill that little bastard on Halloween!"

Herman woke up sweating in his orphanage bed from the night terrors. The voodoo curse corrupted Herman's mind throughout his bad dream. Herman gave in to the voice of his father. This was the start of his downfall as a human being.

Herman's mother was a prostitute who was embarrassed when she became impregnated by a clown. She took no responsibility for raising Herman. Herman knew his father only during his childhood. He became a carnival hustler and followed in his father's clown footsteps. Herman found ways to earn money, even when public events weren't occurring. Herman was a true hustler. He set up his booth all over the streets of Ireland and cheated the innocent.

Herman's father had passed away from liver failure as a result of alcoholism. Alcoholism was a serious problem in the McRandle family. As a matter of fact, Herman was intoxicated as he sat at his booth. As Herman waited to rip off a customer, he rudely shouted, "Hey, nice bust, you whore!" as a woman with giant breasts strutted by. The woman with the giant breasts gave him a look of utter disgust and walked away.

McRandle said, "Come on, folks! Don't be shy! Step right up and give it a try! It's your lucky night at the Dublin Halloween Fair!"

Moments later, an Irishman walked over to Herman's crooked booth with curiosity. This curious Irishman went by the name of Jonny Kerrigan. Kerrigan was a short and stubborn man who loved to gamble. Jonny decided to use all that was left of his spare change to give Herman's game a try.

Herman ran a crooked card game at the fair. He had fast hands when he shuffled a deck of cards. The sneaky card-shuffling trick he used was a subtle motion—McRandle would always skim his left hand slightly slower than his right hand while shuffling. This unique shuffling motion caused certain cards to remain on top of the deck. Five black-suited cards remained on the top. It was a deceptive shuffling trick that Herman learned from his late father.

Herman would then place three cards face down, not revealing their color. Herman knew that all three of the cards he placed down were black. The con artist aspect of this game was that Herman's catchphrase was, "It's not that hard to pick the red card." That weasel McRandle had been scamming honest, hardworking folks for years with his shabby tricks.

As McRandle collected the coins from Kerrigan, he started to shuffle the deck of cards the shady way his father had taught him. Kerrigan watched the way that Herman shuffled the deck. Although the motion was subtle, Kerrigan noticed a slight delay in McRandle's left hand. Kerrigan thought for a split second that the game might be fixed. Kerrigan was a heavy gambler who loved to play poker, so he knew a shady shuffle when he saw one. Kerrigan still decided to play the game and pick a card at random.

Herman placed three cards from the top of the deck face down on the table. The clown said, "Are you ready, mate? It's not that hard to pick the red card. Take your time or make it quick. Either way, just take your pick." Kerrigan picked the card that was in the middle of the three.

Kerrigan pointed to the table and said, "The card in the middle, please, sir."

When Herman flipped the card over, the color was black. Herman said, "Sorry, buddy, that wasn't your round. How about another try?"

Kerrigan had already lost most of his money gambling earlier that night, and he was in a pretty foul mood. Jonny had just used the last of his coins to play McRandle's crooked game. Jonny quickly flipped over the other two cards and saw that they were both black. Kerrigan pointed at McRandle and yelled, "You cheated me, you crooked clown! I demand a full refund!"

Herman said, "No refunds. Maybe next time there will be three lucky red cards on the table. Come on! Wipe that grin off your face and give it another try!"

Kerrigan gave a disgruntled look at McRandle and shouted, "I'm broke because you ripped me off!" Kerrigan gave McRandle a vicious right jab to his big, green clown nose. Herman was dazed for a second as he prepared to fight back. McRandle struck back with a vicious headbutt that put Kerrigan on the ground in agony as Herman laughed maliciously over his fallen enemy.

As Kerrigan prepared to get up, Herman grasped for his chest in some kind of attack preparation. On Herman's chest was a necklace holding a green flower-like emblem. This icon contained a flammable liquid that McRandle prepared just for such an instance as this. As Kerrigan got up, Herman grabbed one of the decorative torches that were scattered around the fair. He put the torch in front of his chest while he pressed the flower containing the flammable liquid, creating a jet of flame that he aimed in Kerrigan's direction. The flame struck him on the chest and worked its way around his body, leaving no inch of his body unaffected.

As Kerrigan burned to death, McRandle smiled as he formulated a getaway route in his head. Herman desperately tried to make his getaway, but he could not run fast with the heavy green shoes he was wearing. An angry mob of citizens beat him down, and the citizens punched him in the face repeatedly.

Two constables quickly got involved and controlled the crowd. Officers Burnes and Nolan blew their whistles in an attempt to get the angry mob to stand down. The mob stood down as Burnes and Nolan pulled out their police clubs. They both let loose and whacked Herman's goofy-looking green body a few times. As the police managed to put him in handcuffs, Herman shouted, "Fuck, I'm captured!"

This bizarre incident put all eyes on Herman. Children at the fair were crying because they thought that a clown was supposed to be funny, not evil. McRandle held his head down in shame as officers Burnes and Nolan walked him over to a police cage connected to a horse-drawn carriage. After Herman was placed in the cage, the officers walked back over to the curious crowd. Officer Burnes yelled out to the crowd, "The carnival is closed for the evening. Everyone, please evacuate the premises immediately!" Other officers were attempting to get the fairgoers to evacuate the premises. Some people instantly ran away while others still watched in horror. Officer Nolan became infuriated over the situation. He had a lot of stress going on in his life outside of work. His wife and newborn son were in the hospital. His wife, Molly, was having health complications after recently giving birth to their child last week. She had a rare and undiagnosed infection in her uterus and needed very costly medical treatment by trustworthy doctors at the Dublin Memorial Hospital. His son, Tyler, was born just last week. Tyler was born a month prematurely, so his bones and organs were still a little underdeveloped. Tyler was undergoing medical treatment at the Dublin Memorial Hospital, which was also very costly. Officer Nolan was worried about his wife and son. He wanted to be there for them, but his shift ended at midnight. Not being there for them, and the recent murder at the fair had him riled up. Officer Nolan shouted out to the crowd, "The fuckin' carnival is closed, you goddamn morons! Go the fuck home right now, or else I'll start clubbing people who are too fuckin' stupid to get the message!"

The fairgoers who had heard Officer Nolan's recent threat had gotten the hell out of there quickly. Other fairgoers eventually scattered from the fair as the carnies closed down their crooked operations for the evening.

**

The wagon transported the clown a few miles up the road to the Dublin Mental Institution. Burnes and Nolan were officers at the institution who had been assigned to public duties for the Dublin Halloween Fair. They'd been working at the institution for twelve years. They were both rugged Irishmen and very experienced constables. They had both been builders before they became officers. These men constructed the Dublin Mental Institution's juvenile facility. When Burnes and Nolan had met the warden of the facility, they had formed an immediate friendship. The warden had been very impressed with the architectural design of the juvenile facility. He thought the whole crew had done an excellent job. The warden had convinced Burnes and Nolan to join the Dublin authority force.

Within a year, Burnes and Nolan gave up their jobs as construction workers. The warden personally trained them and hired them as constables at his facility. He felt as though they would be an asset to the establishment. Burnes and Nolan had served proudly for the last twelve years. In their twelve years on the force, they had become more arrogant and occasionally corrupt.

Herman was irate, but strangely enough, he sat very patiently in the back of the wagon. Herman said to the officers, "I'm going to bust out of this prison tonight and cause a ruckus in these fuckin' woods!"

Officer Nolan looked back at Herman and said, "We will shoot you if you cause any problems with us or the other mental patients."

The clown said, "I would love to eat a bullet! After I die, I'll fuck with you in the afterlife!"

Officer Nolan lit a cigar and said, "Whatever, you stupid, wimpy clown."

The clown said, "Hey, can I score a cigar?"

Officer Nolan said, "Sorry, you're shit out of luck, clown. Now shut the hell up back there, or I'll fuckin' club you again!"

McRandle sat quietly with his evil thoughts as the chariot headed slowly to the institution.

CHAPTER 4

Back on the Dublin trails, Charles O'Callahan, also known as Evil Chef Scumbag, was preparing his station for the big stew. Charles O'Callahan was a former mental patient at the Dublin Mental Institution. He was a man of a heavy frame and was forty-eight years old. He had a passion for reckless cooking and a big appetite.

He'd been an unsanitary, stubborn chef at the Dublin Elementary School until he lost his job and his mind. O'Callahan had gotten into an argument with his coworker, Jerry O'Riley, and murdered him in front of the students after O'Riley had disagreed with O'Callahan's culinary methods. O'Riley did not like the way O'Callahan butchered the cows; he thought that the food the children ate should be treated properly. Obviously, O'Callahan did not agree, and he butchered Jerry on June 12, 1875.

This act of murder, which happened on the last day of the school year, was a terrible thing for the school children to witness before they started their summer vacation. They all had a look of horror on their little faces when O'Riley bled to death on the dirty kitchen floor.

Charles O'Callahan served fifteen years in the Dublin Mental Institution for this act of human slaughter. He served as the head chef at the institution for the fifteen years he was imprisoned. He was allowed back into society on June 12, 1890, and he joined the evil tribal cult of the Dublin Woods. The cult proudly took this man in for his culinary value. He resided in a small shack in the Dublin Woods right near his unsanitary workstation. Charles was the head chef of the haunted trail. He cooked meals for all the lunatics residing in the Dublin Woods. He often received vegetable donations from the crazed farmer O'Sullivan.

The eastern section of the trails was where former mental patients roamed for animals and trespassers. This particular group of former mental patients worked under the command of O'Callahan. Once a person or small animal was captured it was usually thrown into a cage. A few raccoons were transferred from the cage into O'Callahan's stew. O'Callahan and his companions had tendencies toward cannibalism. They loved the taste of a raccoon or a trespasser in O'Callahan's stew. These former mental patients strongly guarded the no-trespassing zone.

Holly and Harold McBrier, a married couple, walked past their house in the backwoods of Dublin. They were both dressed up as green pirates and wore black pirate hats and black patches over their left eyes. They both enjoyed Halloween in a festive way and couldn't stand the sadistic side of it. They held hands as they enjoyed their walk.

Holly and Harold were very peaceful people and had both been raised to treat people with respect. The McBriers were a small couple—they both stood just under five feet tall, and each had short, dark brown hair. The McBriers took pride in their Protestant faith.

Harold had proposed marriage to Holly in this particular section of the Dublin Woods the previous year on Halloween night. They wanted to have a celebration one year later in the same section of the woods, wearing the same Halloween costumes. They wanted to get out of the house and have a romantic picnic in the woods where Harold had proposed. The couple had common sense and knew not to walk much further into the Dublin Woods.

They stopped walking about a quarter of a mile outside of the no-trespassing section of Dublin, then to the exact spot where the proposal had taken place. Harold put down his picnic basket and took his wife into his arms. They began to kiss as they slowly dropped to the ground and got more comfortable.

One of O'Callahan's guards had wandered past the no-trespassing section in pursuit of Patrican. What this ill-minded person heard from a distance was the couple making noises. When he approached, he saw them kissing on the ground. He lost focus on Patrican and roamed back to where more of his companions were. The guard said to his companions, "There's two lurking trespassers in the forest, fooling around on the grass, just outside the no-trespassing section! If they've seen the trespasser, then they might be able to point us in his direction. Let's head over there right now and question them before they're gone. We'll hear what they have to say before we torture them. Come on, men, follow me this way!" The other guards immediately followed their evil companion down the path. Within a few minutes, five men from O'Callahan's crew swarmed over to the public section to disturb the romance.

The McBriers thought that they would be safe as long as they didn't roam too deep into the Dublin Woods, but they had made a bad judgment call and compromised their safety. O'Callahan's crewmembers swarmed them. The McBrier's looked at the guards and weren't that nervous at first, but they were curious as to why the guards had approached them. The guard who had spotted them kissing in the forest said to the McBriers, "Excuse me, folks, I'm sorry to disturb the two of you, but I have a question, and maybe one of you might have an answer for me."

"What is your question, sir?" asked Harold.

"Have you seen a trespasser roaming around here?" asked the guard.

"No. We haven't seen anyone else roaming around here, sir," said Harold.

"I haven't seen anyone else roaming around here, either," said Holly a few seconds later. The guards all gave hostile looks toward the McBriers. The McBriers became suspicious of these guards and there was a very awkward silence for a few seconds, as all these people stood in the forest.

"Why do you ask, sir?" asked Holly.

"He murdered a few of my companions tonight and we're trying to capture him before he escapes the forest. Once we capture him, we are going to seek justice and execute him for his sins," said the guard.

Holly responded, "I'm sorry, sir. I wish we could help you, but we haven't seen anyone else roaming around here tonight. I'm sorry about your companions getting murdered out here tonight. Perhaps you can get the local authorities involved in this rather than trying to seek justice for yourselves. Violence is wrong."

"But what about vigilante justice, my friends?" asked the guard.

"Vigilante justice is wrong as well, sir," replied Holly.

"Yes. I agree with you, honey, that any kind of violence is wrong. Hopefully, this will all get resolved peacefully," replied Harold.

"The two of you aren't lying to me, are you?" asked the guard.

"No. We're not lying to you, sir," said Harold.

"And what about you? Are you lying to me, bitch?" asked the guard.

"No, sir. I'm not lying to you," said Holly with tears in her eyes.

The guard replied back to the McBriers, "I don't believe you. The two of you are lying to me so that you can help this trespasser escape from the forest. I'm going to ask you this one more fuckin' time, and one of you better tell me something useful. Where the fuck is the trespasser?"

"We don't know where this person is!" shouted Holly with tears in her eyes as she nervously spoke back to this evil man.

"My wife is very upset right now, sir, and I'm sorry that we can't help you on this. Again, we honestly have no idea where this person that you're looking for is right now."

"I don't believe your filthy lies. Both of you will be punished. Tie them both up and drag them to O'Callahan's prep station so they can be executed for their sins!" shouted the guard.

The nervous McBriers got pinned down face-first in the dirt and tied up with their hands behind their backs. The helpless couple yelled and screamed for help, so the guards tied cloths around their mouths. The McBriers were now completely unable to scream for help. Evil was among them, and no one was around to save them from it. They tried to shake their way free and escape, but both failed, and their attempts enraged the guards even more. The guards yanked them off the ground and forced them to O'Callahan's prep station of death. The treacherous walk from the picnic to O'Callahan's station took about three minutes.

Evil Chef Scumbag waited to cook them in the stew. The chef said, "No need to throw these two lurking trespassers in the cage! The stew is ready for them! The taste of two trespassers along with O'Sullivan's vegetables will make a hearty broth! Ladies first!"

The chef pointed his dirty knife right at Holly. The guards dragged Holly over to the chef, who forced Holly to lie down face up. She was strapped to the center of the evil chef's prep station. O'Callahan removed the cloth from her mouth. Holly screamed. "Shut the fuck up, bitch!" shouted O'Callahan. Holly's husband watched as O'Callahan beheaded her with a butcher knife. Her head was tossed into the stew as Harold grieved for the loss of his soulmate.

Holly's body was hacked up by the evil chef and thrown into the horrible stew. O'Callahan pointed his bloody knife at Harold and said, "Now it's time for you to share the same fate as your wife, you forbidden trespasser!"

O'Callahan's crew of guards threw Harold onto the chef's cutting board. He suffered the same process as his wife before him. Evil Chef Scumbag and his motley crew of evil guards laughed as they executed a couple completely innocent of trespassing.

CHAPTER 5

On the northern peak of the trail, three young punks hiked up the back section of the mountain to cause mischief to the hermit residing atop. These three boys were all Dublin locals and were twelve years old. Their names were Robert Flanagan, Dennis Fitzpatrick, and Hank McManis. They all went to school together in Dublin and had a taste for mischief on this crisp Halloween evening. All three of these kids were dressed up in black for their high-mountain mission.

Robert pressured his friends to go on a daring mission atop the mountain with him. He told his friends that a mountain dweller lived on the peak of Dublin Mountain in a small hut. His friends became curious after hearing this news, and they had to see the mysterious mountain dweller with their own eyes. All these Irish children lived within a mile of the mountainside.

Robert lived half a mile away from the mountainside in a small house with his family. His family had remained safe from the curses of the Dublin Woods for as long as they had resided nearby. Robert was the only child of Christopher and Francine Flanagan. Francine and her husband owned Flanagan's Pub in downtown Dublin. Their pub had been in service for twenty years. They were both forty-five years old and cherished their only son, who worked as a busboy at Flanagan's and did chores for his family after school.

The local drunks at Flanagan's thought that Robert was adorable. Robert was courteous and attentive as a busboy. However, outside of his busboy duties at Flanagan's, Robert was a little renegade. For the past week, Robert had been sneaking out past his bedtime and roaming the northern peak of the mountain. The lunatics who roamed the Dublin Woods focused none of their manpower on the trails lining the mountainside.

The hermit was sleeping when the children wandered onto his territory. Unlike the other lunatics in the Dublin Woods, the hermit had never been a mental patient. He was an angry mountain dweller who hated trespassers. The guards never bothered the hermit, and the hermit never bothered them. There was mutual respect between the hermit and the mentally ill.

The hermit, Othello Hanlon, had long, grungy hair and a scruffy brown beard. He was filthy and refused to bathe in the Dublin River down below the mountain. His stench was unbearable. Conceived atop Dublin Mountain, he had lived there all his life. He was raised to be a hermit from the day he was conceived.

Robert Flanagan brought his schoolbag containing a carton of eggs and a set of bolt cutters. Robert opened his bag and took out the items, which he showed off to his friends. His friends were amazed when they saw the bolt cutters and the carton of eggs.

Robert said to his friends, "I've been staking this place out all week. Let's egg this fuckin' mountain dweller." Robert used the bolt cutters to cut a crawl space through the barbed-wire fence. A sudden change of emotion happened among Robert's friends. They both got a bad feeling about the high, dark mountain mission.

 "Something about this place seems a little off to me," Dennis said. "The mountain dweller who lives up here probably doesn't want us vandalizing his territory. For all we know, the mountain dweller could be a complete psychopath."

Hank replied, "I think you're right, Dennis. This place seems a little sketchy. Pissing off this mountain dweller could turn out ugly for us. We don't know who he is or what he's capable of. We don't belong up here. We should head back down the mountain and go home. Or we could go back to the fair and try to win our money back from that crazy clown."

Robert yelled, "Don't you two back down on this mission! We didn't climb up all this way just for nothing! I say we egg this fuckin' mountain dweller and send a message! We don't want this shithead dwelling on our mountain! I'm almost finished with the crawlspace! Let's go, girls! We don't have all night!"

After a few more minutes with the bolt cutters, the crawlspace was formed. Hank and Dennis gave in to Robert's peer pressure because they didn't want to seem afraid. The three punks could now access the evil hermit's property. They crawled through the perimeter and entered the hermit's lair. The three little renegades grabbed the eggs from the carton and began bombarding the hermit's rotting shack. A barrage of eggs hit the hermit's shack.

The hermit awakened from his sleep and stepped outside of his small hut. He stared down at the three troublemakers and shouted, "Who dares disturb me in my slumber?!"

Robert shouted at the hermit, "I hate you, you fuckin' bum! We don't want you living in Dublin! Get the hell off our mountain!" Then he picked up a rock and threw it at the hermit's head.

Robert had just taken the practical joke to a whole new level. Robert and his friends laughed for a few seconds as if they had won a territorial dispute against the hermit and demoralized him. Othello, however, wasn't demoralized at all. He was more enraged than he'd ever been before. The hermit looked down at the three troublemakers and shouted, "Big mistake, you little bastards! Dublin Mountain is my domain! You're all fuckin' dead!"

The hermit leaped off his small porch and lunged at Robert. Othello grabbed a rock he saw on the ground and bashed it on Robert's face. Robert experienced a devastating blow to the side of his skull and was now completely unconscious. Hank and Dennis witnessed their friend's serious injury and were both frozen in fear. The hermit looked angrily at Hank and Dennis as he pointed his dirty finger toward them both. He got up and hunted them down.

Dennis said in a panic, "Back to the fuckin' crawlspace!"

Dennis and Hank turned their frozen fear into rapid movement. They both made a desperate attempt to flee the hermit's lair, but the hermit eventually caught up with them, just a few feet away from the crawlspace. When he did, he bashed both of their skulls together. This blow knocked them both unconscious.

It took a few minutes, but the hermit managed to gather up all three of the unconscious children. Then Othello grabbed a rope and tied them to a tree. The evil hermit gathered rocks, sticks, and leaves to form a fire pit. The hermit struck a match and started to light the fire pit.

Seconds later, a fire was lit directly under the three bound children. They regained consciousness and realized they were all burning. The children panicked and cried as they realized they were being burned to death. The hermit cackled and said, "Happy Halloween, you little bastards! Welcome to your new grave!"

The three boys burned to death.

The hermit grabbed a filthy blanket he kept outside and used it to smother the fire and the burning children. He pulled apart the burnt rope, untied the three children from the tree, and dragged them one by one toward his gate. The hermit raised his hands in the air and gave a chant to open the evil gate: "Oh mighty gate of Dublin Mountain, I command you to open!"

A sudden bolt of heat lightning created by the mummy struck through the air, and the gate slowly started to open.

As the gate fully opened, the hermit rolled the dead children one by one down a slope of the mountain. The slope led to a two-thousand-foot drop onto a lower section of the Dublin trail. The dead children's bodies took about fifteen seconds to fall before landing brutally on level ground. The hermit's gate slowly closed above as wolves began to devour the flesh of the three burned children.

CHAPTER 6

During the massive manhunt for Mick Patrican, Scott McArthur headed over to Patrick O'Sullivan's garden to inform him of all the chaos going on in the forest tonight. When he arrived there, O'Sullivan had seen him through his dust-stained window. O'Sullivan opened the door of his shack and let him in. "What's up," O'Sullivan said.

"There is chaos in the forest tonight, and we've received some harsh blowback from a feisty trespasser. The trespasser just killed O'Neill and O'Connor a little while ago, in retaliation of our evil cult. I've got all our men searching for the trespasser as we speak. All I want from you right now is for you to stay put right here in your shack and keep a close eye on your property line for trespassers. I gave my wife a savage beating earlier in the evening because she can't cook for shit. If you happen to spot my wife attempting to escape from the forest tonight, hold her at gunpoint and force her to walk back home. If she gives you any shit, don't shoot her, but threaten to, just to get her to listen to your demands. I only want you to shoot her if she fails to listen to several of your warnings. Is that clear, you fuckin' idiot?" said McArthur. "Yes, sir," replied O'Sullivan. After the conversation ended, McArthur headed back into the Dublin Woods to help his companions search for the fugitive. Patrick O'Sullivan stayed in his shack and looked out of his dust-stained window for trespassers.

**

On the mountainside, a few miles away from the hermit's lair, was the Dublin Mental Institution. The Dublin Mental Institution was a highly secured prison for mental defectives who were over the age of eighteen. This institution contained lunatics, as did the Dublin Woods. The only difference was that these mental patients were confined away from society. Construction on the Dublin Mental Institution was fully completed on August 22, 1850. The architects involved in the construction made several mistakes along the way and eventually fixed them, and several builders injured themselves during the exhausting construction. The construction of the building posed many problems throughout the building process.

The construction of the Dublin Mental Institution began on October 8, 1849. On Halloween night, 1849, two construction workers named Frank Larson and Virgil O'Maley were working on the basement level of the facility. Their foreman, Mr. McClaren, was giving Frank and Virgil a hard time about the lack of progress they had made so far.

"You two knuckleheads need to quit fuckin' around and get some work done. The basement isn't even dug out yet. You idiots are going to be fired unless you show me some progress and dig this damn space out!" shouted Mr. McClaren before walking away.

Frank was very riled up about the talking-to. Once Mr. McClaren left, Frank told his coworker exactly how he felt. "How can that asshole say that? We work our asses off, and we have only been down at this level of the building for a few days. It's going to take us a few weeks to dig this out ourselves. If he gave us two more workers like I requested yesterday, then we might be able to get the fuckin' job done in a week."

"Just try to calm down, Frank," replied Virgil.

Little did Virgil know that Frank dealt with serious anxiety, which can lead to paranoia and hallucinations. The stress of the job and the reaction of the foreman to their work ethic led Frank into a serious panic episode. While Virgil continued digging, Frank wandered off to try and calm down his panic attack. He began hallucinating intensely and lost all sense of where he was and what he was doing. He walked up to the main floor where the foreman was writing a few things and taking some measurements. He appeared to Frank as a bluish figure, almost a blur, and he appeared to be extraterrestrial. Frank panicked and grabbed a hammer nearby.

As Frank approached his boss, the foreman looked at Frank and began yelling profanities. "Get back to work right now, Larson, or you're fuckin' fired!" shouted Mr. McClaren. Mr. McClaren put up his hands in defense. Frank began to whack his boss several times in the skull with the hammer. He had no idea that he was bludgeoning his boss to death as he hammered the bluish figure. When he was done, he dropped the hammer and went back to work. This murder was only the beginning of the bloodbaths this facility would eventually endure.

**

There was a mandatory twenty-four-hour lockdown for all convicted prisoners. This mandatory lockdown rule also stood for volunteer patients who'd committed themselves to the institution. The prisoners were denied the privilege of breathing fresh air, although they could see it through the barred windows. The prisoners ate the food provided in the cafeteria, while the staff members at the facility were privileged to get served higher quality food which was provided by the medical staff. The security features in the building were very advanced. The state-of-the-art security features made escape from the premises very difficult. Privileged officers on duty at the institution possessed master prison keys. These keys were able to lock and unlock the main doorways and all the cells. Each cell had a small bathroom. Each bathroom was equipped with a toilet, a faucet, and a shower. Although individual cells stayed unlocked during lockdown, access in and out of the building was prohibited. Inmates' rooms were locked only if they were confined to solitary.

The Dublin Mental Institution had a haunting history. An evil ghost known as the Ghost of Cornelius floated high in the air over the cursed asylum as McRandle approached from a distance. This evil ghost floated by as a warning sign that things were about to go from bad to worse. There was a myth that a friendly spirit was able to place a boundary on the wanderings of the Ghost of Cornelius. A few Irish folks believed that a friendly spirit had trapped the Ghost of Cornelius in the Dublin Woods and spared the rest of Ireland.

The Irish myth about a friendly spirit fighting off the evil curse of the Dublin Woods was true. The friendly spirit was the ghost of General Butch McPherson, an Irish soldier who fought in the battle against Egyptian soldiers two thousand years ago. Thousands of men died in this relentless war that had spawned over two magical four-leaf clovers believed to be so powerful that, if fused together, the magic produced could either be used to heal or destroy Ireland. General McPherson was the lone survivor of this violent war. It took McPherson and his crew a decade to build underground traps in a cave and prepare for this war. General McPherson almost got trapped in the cave while searching for the magical four-leaf clover he had once possessed. He had lost this magical clover in the cave while he was battling with the mummy. The mummy had one of these magical clovers implanted in its heart. The mummy went after McPherson because it wanted the second clover. General McPherson did everything he could to defend himself against the evil mummy and protect his clover. McPherson stabbed the mummy in its evil heart with a sword and stunned it. He had thought that he killed the mummy by doing this, but he was wrong. The mummy was only stunned by this sword strike. General McPherson eventually found his way out of this hellish cave, carrying the mummy's corpse with him. But his clover was lost somewhere inside the cave. McPherson dragged the mummy's corpse uphill and buried it in a ditch. There was an unmarked tombstone next to the ditch. McPherson buried the mummy in a ditch two thousand years ago, on Halloween night. The evil clover in the mummy's heart had rejuvenated the blood vessels in its heart and the mummy was still alive because of this magical power. The mummy comes alive every Halloween night, desperately searching for the missing clover. The clover has been lost in this cave for two thousand years.

Cornelius had been an Irishman before he died. Cornelius Walsh and Michael Patrican had been the two most experienced fishermen in all of Ireland, and they had been rival fishermen for almost a decade. In October of 1850, Cornelius and Michael had sailed the seas of Northern Ireland on separate missions in hopes of finding a promising school of fish. Cornelius had no luck at all. He had sailed toward the coastline, hoping that his luck would change. After having no such luck, he docked his boat on the sand and took a hiatus from fishing.

Michael had a successful day of fishing, but he eventually ran out of live bait. He had been a few miles away from the shoreline when he headed toward land to gather up more bait. Michael had noticed a small fishing vessel beached on the sand. He was curious about the boat for a few seconds before turning his attention to the job of getting more bait. He had no idea the fishing boat belonged to his enemy.

When Michael approached the small shoreline, he anchored his vessel on the edge of the coastline next to a giant rock. After he secured his boat, he grabbed his minnow trap and stepped off his boat. When both of his feet hit the Irish sand, he saw his enemy eye to eye for the first time.

Michael Patrican saw his rival for only a split-second before he was blindsided and killed by him. Cornelius had hidden behind a giant rock off the shoreline when he noticed Michael's vessel approaching and remained hidden behind the rock while Michael docked. Cornelius had crept quietly around the rock with a small knife in his right hand. Cornelius gave Michael no time to react when he came from behind the rock and slit his throat.

On the night of October 11, 1850, Michael Patrican was murdered. He was also decapitated, and Cornelius had taken his head upon fleeing. Michael was the Patrican brothers' grandfather. The brothers never met their grandfather because he died before they were all conceived.

After Cornelius Walsh murdered his enemy, he set sail on his fishing boat and fled the area. Not long after he set sail, a couple, George and Mindy Kelly, walked along the beach not far from where the murder had occurred. The Kellys had met on this beach in their early childhood and became the best of friends. They had met when they were five years old and had grown up on the beach together. The beach was still their favorite spot to spend their leisure time.

The beach was five miles long, and in the midst of their travels, they noticed a murdered man on the ground next to a fishing boat. "Oh, Jesus!" shouted Mindy as she pointed toward the dead body. "Look over there, George! That poor person is fuckin' decapitated!" George looked over toward the dead body lying on the sand. "Let's get the fuck out of here, right now, Mindy, and report this to the authorities."

Within minutes, the authorities organized a massive search in hopes of catching the murderer. Twelve constables searched the beach and the northern Irish Sea. Six constables searched the beach, and the other six constables took a vessel and searched the sea. When the constables had sailed ten miles offshore, they spotted a man rowing a small boat in the middle of the ocean. The man the constables spotted was Cornelius Walsh.

When he knew the constables had spotted him, Cornelius started paddling as hard as he could. The six constables rowed their vessel much faster than Cornelius could, and they gained on him. When the constables had rowed within one hundred feet of their target, two of them pulled out shotguns and opened fire on Cornelius.

Cornelius heard shots being fired at him and abandoned the ship. He dove into the ocean and tried to swim away. Cornelius's small fishing boat was struck with a few bullets as the constables missed their target. Two of the constables jumped into the sea to try and capture their fleeing suspect. The four other constables watched and waited for their suspect to emerge from the ocean.

Cornelius had been underwater for about a minute when he ran out of breath and emerged from the cold swells of the choppy Irish ocean. When he emerged, the two constables were within ten feet of him. They swam toward him quickly and managed to apprehend him. Walsh tried to fight off the two constables and swim away, but he was unsuccessful. The constables searched Walsh's boat and found Michael Patrican's decapitated head. Cornelius Walsh was found guilty of the murder of Michael Patrican and was sentenced to the Dublin Mental Institution for twenty years. He was the first man ever committed to the Dublin Mental Institution. He served nineteen of those twenty years and died of natural causes at the age of fifty-four on Halloween 1869.

Since death, the Ghost of Cornelius had been haunting the cemetery of this cursed asylum on Halloween night, seeking revenge for the years it was confined to the asylum.

CHAPTER 7

The police wagon arrived at the Dublin Mental Institution. Burnes and Nolan walked to the back of the cage and opened the back latch. They noticed that the clown was passed out and drunk as a skunk. Officer Nolan pulled out his baton. He quietly whispered to his partner, "I'm going to club this goofy bastard one more time just because it's Halloween."

With his club, Officer Nolan viciously struck Herman's ribcage. The clown felt the fierce blow, gasped for air, and slowly got up.

Burnes said to Nolan, "You always were a class act." Burnes and Nolan both sneered because the clown was a scumbag. The two of them slowly escorted the shackled clown inside the Dublin Mental Institution and down the hallway into the criminal processing room of the facility. Thomas Roberts, the warden of the Dublin Mental Institution and the juvenile facility, waited in the office. He served as a guidance counselor for mental patients and determined the fate of prisoners with parole hearings. His father, the previous warden at the Dublin Mental Institution, had died on September 16, 1872, and left the position to Thomas in the family will. Thomas had buried his father behind the institution.

From then on, constables who passed away were buried behind the Dublin Mental Institution in a gated cemetery in honor of their service. Thomas was a constable at the institution when his father was in charge. He and his father spent many days and nights at a private shooting facility within the institution. Thomas and his father both had developed long-distance shooting skills through years of practice, but ultimately, they had a knack for it. Thomas was a corrupt warden who wasn't afraid to occasionally break the regulations of the institution.

Burnes and Nolan escorted the clown into Dr. Roberts's office. As Dr. Roberts and McRandle stared each other in the face, there was a moment of awkward silence. Dr. Roberts said, "Herman McRandle. We meet at last. I'm glad you're here. Society can do without you. Welcome to the Dublin Mental Institution."

McRandle stood there with a disgruntled look on his white face.

Officer Burnes said to the warden, "Sir, this man is guilty of murder. He burned an innocent man to death at the Dublin Halloween Fair. He was captured before he could escape."

"Good job, gentlemen," the warden said, "I knew I could count on you."

Officer Burnes said, "The angry mob at the fair deserves half the credit as well, sir. They captured him before we did."

The warden replied, "I'm sure they do, Officer Burnes. Their bravery, along with their successful efforts in restraining this lunatic, is much appreciated."

The warden said to McRandle, "I've seen your profile, Mr. McRandle, and I've talked to other prison wardens all over Ireland. They warned me about your bullshit, and we won't stand for it in this institution. There's no trial or freedom for you anymore. Your days of hustling innocent folks at the Dublin Halloween Fair are long gone."

Dr. Roberts cleared his throat, then continued, "Herman McRandle, you are hereby sentenced to the Dublin Mental Institution for life. You will report to your cell on the fifth floor, cell number 499. You are the only criminal residing on the top level. We have stairwells at all four corners of the building. We have a strict policy in this institution. There is a mandatory twenty-four-hour lockdown for all convicted prisoners. Our facility holds five hundred rooms. However, there are approximately two hundred mental defectives currently serving time here. I don't want you causing any trouble, McRandle. That's why I'm secluding you.

"The cafeteria is open for five more minutes, and then the warning bell will ring. After the bell rings, you have five minutes to report to your assigned cell. You act up once, and I'll personally put a bullet in your skull. Remember, Mr. McRandle, we have the guns, and you're a piece of dog shit. I dare you to make a move."

McRandle decided to be a wise guy, so he said, "Whatever you say, sunshine."

"Do I detect a tone of sarcasm, Mr. McRandle?" asked Dr. Roberts. "Just so you know, we frown upon that kind of shit here."

McRandle started to become angry again.

"Fuck you and your bullshit rules, Roberts!" Herman replied. "I plead insanity! I dare you to pull the fuckin' trigger! When I die, my evil spirit will live on and fuck with your sanity!"

Dr. Roberts said, "I don't believe in ridiculous superstitions involving ghosts and evil spirits, Mr. McRandle. Officer Nolan, club this pitiful clown a few times and get him the fuck out of my sight."

"With pleasure, sir."

Officer Nolan whacked the clown with his baton three times as Herman screamed in pain and braced himself. "Thank you, Officer Nolan," said Dr. Roberts. "You just made my night. I need another quick favor as well. I need you and Officer Burnes to check on

Samuel McTavish. Please make sure that he gets his food and his medicine."

The officers simultaneously said, "Yes, sir, Dr. Roberts." Burnes and Nolan escorted the clown out of Dr. Roberts's office and down the main hallway. The two officers used their keys to take the shackles off the clown.

Officer Burnes said to Herman, "Remember what Dr. Roberts said about our strict policy? Don't you try to pull any bullshit, McRandle. We're the ones who are in control now."

Officer Nolan said, "The cafeteria is straight ahead, and you have five minutes to get something to eat. Oh, by the way, the food sucks here."

Herman walked toward the cafeteria with a shit-eating grin on his face as he slowly turned his clown head back and said, "Hey, Burnes, Nolan, I'm bullshlt about those club attacks. I'll get my revenge when you both least expect it."

The officers shrugged off McRandle's threat and calmly walked away.

**

Herman entered the cafeteria just before the mental patients were no longer allowed. As he approached the greasy chef, he looked at him and said, "Hey, greaseball, let me get some corned beef and some of those shitty-looking mashed potatoes. I'm starving."

The greasy chef served the clown exactly what he had asked for. McRandle accepted his disgusting plate of food from the scummy chef and sat down at an empty table. Many of the mental patients were obsessively gazing at him. His clown outfit made him the center of attention. The cafeteria was very quiet, with the exception of the soft whispers of raving lunatics. His recent arrival at the institution made the mental patients extremely curious.

McRandle was a good con artist, and he wasn't even hungry at all. What McRandle did was very clever and sneaky. He managed to pocket a metal fork that was provided with his meal. Herman looked around the cafeteria and noticed that other mental patients were staring at him. Herman said, "Fear no evil, men! Burnes and Nolan are going to die tonight!"

The mentally ill around the room were all in shock to hear what McRandle had to say. No more than a few minutes later, the bell rang and feeding time for the prisoners was over.

Of all the mental patients, one man was now truly afraid. The petrified man who overheard McRandle's threats was Walter McFrancis, a thirty-year-old paranoid schizophrenic who feared the everyday world. He was a frail-boned man with light brown hair. He was very easily intimidated when he witnessed or experienced any kind of danger. Walter had turned himself into this institution voluntarily after his mother died when he was twenty-eight. He had never known his father because the man abandoned him when he needed a father figure.

Being around his mother all the time had turned him into a big mama's boy. When she passed away, he had not been able to care for himself properly. Although Walter was physically healthy, he suffered from mental illness, and he also suffered from a severe case of insomnia. He had decided it was best for him to now reside here. Most of the inmates at the facility referred to Walter as a pussy. However, McFrancis had never been physically abused by the harassing inmates due to the strict policy enforced by the warden of the facility.

Walter thought there was something very dangerous about the clown, but tried to ignore the situation and block it out of his mind.

While the mental patients were leaving the cafeteria, Burnes and Nolan headed down to the basement science lab to check on Samuel McTavish. Burnes and Nolan had multiple responsibilities during the night's shift. McTavish was a bitter mental patient who caused unnecessary chaos in the cafeteria. On October 1, 1892, Samuel McTavish started a fight with a mental patient named Chester O'Ryan in the cafeteria. Officer Jones had seen McTavish throw his meal at Chester. When McTavish's scrambled eggs and corned beef hash hit O'Ryan square in the face, a massive food fight began.

O'Ryan became enraged over this and charged at McTavish. O'Ryan shoved McTavish off the cafeteria bench and began choking him with his hands. Within a few seconds, McTavish broke free from the chokehold and started throwing punches at O'Ryan's face. O'Ryan took a few punches, but before he was able to throw a few of his own, Officer Jones jumped on top of McTavish to break up the fight.

McTavish had lashed out at Officer Jones instead of submitting to him. Officer Jones had fallen and hit his skull on the cafeteria floor. Officer Jones was injured, and the food fight in the cafeteria got more chaotic. Two dozen constables tried to restrain the patients during the food fight in the cafeteria. Four constables had clubbed McTavish within seconds of Officer Jones's head injury. O'Ryan had been restrained by the constables, but not beaten. Ten more constables soon arrived at the cafeteria for backup. The food fight lasted around five minutes before the constables took control. Officer Jones suffered a mild head injury and missed a few days of work.

Chester O'Ryan was proven not to be at fault for the altercation with McTavish. McTavish was proven to be the one responsible for provoking the food fight, along with the assault on Officer Jones. As punishment, the mental patients had to clean up the mess they had made in the cafeteria. Dr. Roberts then put McTavish in solitary confinement. McTavish was an annoyance—he constantly shouted, "Let me the fuck out of this cage! I'm a human being! You can't treat me like this!"

Dr. Roberts couldn't take McTavish as a problem anymore, so he went against regulations. He had studied science and the traits of human anatomy. He used a tranquilizer to take McTavish down. Once McTavish passed out, Dr. Roberts did illegal scientific tests on him.

According to facility regulations, the normal protocol for punishing a problematic patient was solitary confinement. Dr. Roberts took away Samuel's rights and went against protocol. One could call Dr. Roberts a human devil. Samuel became Dr. Roberts's experimental lab rat. Dr. Roberts had a sinister plan to create a genetically altered human for prison security purposes. Had this experiment been successful, Dr. Roberts's wish would have come to fruition. Instead, Samuel McTavish became permanently disfigured, and he grew a third eye on the left side of his face. His left arm shrank, and his right arm grew to twice its normal size. Samuel McTavish would remain a freak in a cage for the rest of his pitiful life.

Loud noises echoed from below as Burnes and Nolan walked farther down the basement steps. The basement level was extremely dark. Officer Burnes shone a small oil lamp ahead of them as they cautiously walked down the stairwell. The officers reached the bottom steps of the basement.

As they walked toward the secured cage, McTavish shouted, "Officer Burnes, Officer Nolan, you need to release me at once! Dr. Roberts has gone way too far with these illegal experiments on me! My body is changing form, and I can't stop vomiting. I'm nauseous all the time, and it smells horrendous down here. I'm living in my own filth. I'm dizzy, and I have a massive headache. I don't feel right. I'm a human being. You can't treat me like this! I need to breathe fresh air. This cage and this medicine are causing me to go insane. I have my rights. Release me now!"

Officer Burnes said, "You lost your rights when you attacked Officer Jones! You're lucky you're still alive, McTavish!"

Samuel hissed at Burnes and Nolan from inside his dirty cage. There was a disgusting bucket of fish scraps in the basement that had been left there overnight, discarded from last night's dinner. Flies were swarming over the smelly bucket of fish scraps. Officer Burnes grabbed the bucket of fish scraps. Officer Nolan pulled out his police club, clubbed the cage, and said to McTavish, "Stand down, you fuckin' freak." McTavish hissed at the officers again. Officer Nolan clubbed the cage again, then he tucked his club back into his police uniform. Officer Nolan pulled out a tranquilizer gun and pointed it at McTavish. Officer Nolan began to open the cage while still pointing his tranquilizer gun at McTavish.

As McTavish quietly stood down, Officer Nolan opened the cage. As soon as the cage was fully opened, Officer Burnes dumped the bucket containing the fish scraps all over Samuel McTavish. At the exact same time, Officer Nolan shot him with his tranquilizer gun. McTavish immediately passed out after he was shot. This freak show of a man would now be unconscious for about eight hours.

Officer Nolan tucked his tranquilizer gun back into his police uniform and said, "Hey, Burnes, I think that scumbag McTavish was right. It does smell horrendous down here. I'll give this freak a little Halloween shower."

Officer Nolan urinated all over McTavish as he was passed out, unaware of the further abuse. As the two officers began to laugh, Officer Nolan finished urinating on McTavish. Officer Nolan shut the door to the treacherous cage. They gave Samuel McTavish his food and his medicine as Dr. Roberts had requested and finished their corrupt business down in the basement.

They headed back up the long flight of stairs. Officer Burnes was lighting the dark hallway with his lamp. Other prison guards were escorting some of the more dangerous patients back to their cells.

Burnes told Nolan, "I need to track down McRandle and escort him to his cell. The bell rang five minutes ago. I hope he's not clowning around somewhere in the building against our command. If he is, I'll club him again."

"I have to go back to the wagon," Officer Nolan said. "I forgot my cigars in there. Then I'm heading back to my post. I assume you can handle finding that pussy ass clown on your own. If you can't find him, let me know and I'll tell Jones to cover my post and I'll help you find him."

The two of them went their separate ways. Officer Burnes began his search for McRandle on the fifth floor. Once he reached the fifth floor, he briefly checked the hallway and saw no one. After his cursory hallway sweep, he peeked in the closed door of cell number 499. What Officer Burnes saw through the barred window was the illusion of a brilliant con artist—it appeared that the door was closed, and the clown was safely in his cell. Officer Burnes saw a bed in the left corner of the small cell with a bulging blanket and a green clown wig on top of a pillow. As he turned around, he heard a giggle just as he was stabbed in the throat with the pocketed fork.

Herman grabbed the set of keys inside the wounded guard's pocket. Herman opened the door to his assigned cell, grabbed his green clown wig, and put it on his head. Then he dragged the severely injured Officer Burnes into the cell and locked him in. Herman kept the keys on him to make escape impossible for the dying guard.

As Herman started to walk to the stairwell, he knew he had to be sneaky and unseen. Herman managed to walk down the long stairwell with no other officers in sight. All the officers were doing sweeps along the hallways and monitoring the other potentially dangerous prisoners. Once McRandle reached the first floor, he snuck around the corner near the front door of the building. The guard assigned to that section of the first floor was Officer Nolan. He had just returned to his stationed post after grabbing his cigars.

Officer Nolan heard something in the corner of the building and decided to take a quick look. As he looked around the corner, McRandle shouted, "Boo!" and stabbed him in the throat with the stolen fork. The angry clown had vowed his revenge on Burnes and Nolan, who both bled to death. One of McRandle's styles of attack was close kills with a fork. By killing in this manner, he relived a violent moment in his head from his dark childhood past when he killed Thurman McDaniels in the school cafeteria.

McRandle frisked the injured officer and stole his handgun, tucking it into the back of his goofy clown outfit. Walter McFrancis was still up and had witnessed the attack through the barred window of his cell. Walter was terrified and did not make a sound. After stabbing Nolan with the fork, Herman walked to the main door. He inserted the master key into the lock, opened the door, and walked out of the Dublin Mental Institution. McFrancis was the only witness, and the clown didn't even know it.

McFrancis peeked out his barred window and saw the clown vanish into the Dublin Woods. Walter McFrancis started to yell, causing a loud, frantic scene inside his cell. The officer commanding the area just around the corner of the same floor heard the noise Walter was making. Officer Jones ran over from around the corner of the building to see what the noise was about and to investigate the problem.

Once he rounded the corner, he noticed the dead body of Officer Nolan. Officer Jones nervously asked Walter, "Did you see what happened?"

Walter said, "The clown went nuts, killed Officer Nolan, stole his gun, and escaped into the woods. I saw him out my window. I want to talk to Dr. Roberts about this."

Officer Jones said, "Okay, Walter. Try to stay calm. I'll run to his office and inform him of the situation." McFrancis had known Dr. Roberts longer than he had known Officer Jones, so he was much more comfortable speaking with him.

McRandle quickly paced his way a few hundred yards behind the graveyard with his gun drawn as he looked all around for officers in pursuit of him. When he was spooked by a ghost, McRandle recklessly fired his stolen ammunition into the trees.

After McRandle fired six shots toward this glowing figure, the ghost faded away into thin air. The clown's stolen handgun no longer contained ammunition and was rendered useless. McRandle tucked the gun back into his goofy clown outfit. The confused McRandle stood in the woods and gazed at the dark trees as he wondered what the hell it was he had just seen. What the drunken McRandle saw in the trees was a brief glimpse of the Ghost of Cornelius haunting the Dublin Woods.

The Ghost of Cornelius had messed with McRandle's drunken mind. The evil ghost wanted McRandle to fire all his ammunition when it tricked him by mysteriously appearing near the graveyard, and then disappearing. McRandle walked past the graveyard. There were thirty homicidal maniacs searching the forest for Mick Patrican, but these lunatics were not searching near the graveyard, behind the asylum. McRandle entered the haunted trail as he fled further away from the asylum.

**

Officer Jones hustled down the hallway of the facility to Dr. Roberts's office and knocked on the door. Dr. Roberts unlocked the door and said, "What's the matter, Officer Jones?"

Officer Jones replied, "Sir, Officer Nolan is dead, and Officer Burnes is missing. They were on their way to check on McRandle just five minutes ago. I think that McFrancis kid was the only one to see the clown kill Nolan and break out. Walter is a mess, and the clown has escaped into the woods. McRandle stole Officer Nolan's fuckin' gun! We have an emergency on our hands. Walter requested to speak with you about the murder."

Dr. Roberts frantically said, "Search cell number 499 on the fifth floor! Officer Burnes oversaw escorting McRandle to his cell. We need to investigate this mess. I want to speak with Walter before the manhunt for McRandle begins.”

Officer Jones hustled up to the fifth floor as Dr. Roberts headed to the cell containing the paranoid McFrancis. Dr. Roberts knocked on the door of McFrancis’ cell and said, “Walter, it’s me, Dr. Roberts. You said you wanted to speak with me?”

Dr. Roberts entered the cell to have a private conversation with McFrancis. The doctor noticed that Walter was very nervous and breathing awkwardly. The doctor decided to play a mind game with the nervous patient and pretended to be his friend.

Dr. Roberts patted Walter on his shoulder with his right hand. He coddled him and calmly said, “Walter, come take a walk down around the corner to my office. Let me get you a glass of water. You seem thirsty, and this might help calm you down.”

“Thank you, Dr. Roberts,” Walter said. “I need a glass of water. My throat is very dry.”

Walter was still in shock, and hesitant to get up at first. Dr. Roberts said, “It’s okay, Walter. You’re not in any trouble. Come along, now.” The two of them took a walk around the corner and into the office. Walter was still breathing awkwardly. However, he seemed a little calmer than he’d been a few minutes ago. Dr. Roberts said, “Take a seat, Walter.” Walter did so. Roberts continued and said, “Take a few deep breaths, Walter. Let all the air in and out, nice and slow. Try to concentrate on your breathing.” Walter did so. “Excellent, Walter,” said Dr. Roberts.

Roberts poured the patient a glass of water. He walked over to Walter and said, “Take a drink of water, Walter.” Walter grabbed the cup of water from the doctor. Walter began breathing nervously again. He shook a little bit and a small amount of water spilled on the floor. Walter took a few nervous deep breaths, then took a swig of water and coughed. "Excellent, Walter," said Dr. Roberts. "You seem a bit calmer now." Walter cleared his throat and coughed again. "I needed a glass of water, very badly. Thank you, very much for quenching my thirst, Dr. Roberts."

"You're very welcome, my friend. It's an honor to accommodate your important needs here." A few seconds passed. Dr. Roberts continued speaking, "So, Walter, can you tell me what you saw? Don't be nervous. I'm your friend, and I'm here to help you."

Walter said, "I saw the clown stab Officer Nolan with something. After the stabbing, the clown stole Officer Nolan's gun, and Officer Nolan dropped to his death right in front of my eyes. I can't get the horror out of my mind. It was terrible. I saw the clown escape and vanish into the forest from my bedroom window."

Roberts replied, "That's terrible, Walter. Officer Nolan was a good man, and his son was born just last week. I'll have Officer Jones inform his wife. I hate giving good people bad news. As for us, I need you to take a journey with me into the forest. You're the only one who saw the clown."

Walter nervously replied, "Dr. Roberts, I can't face the demons of the dark forest. It gives me the creeps. I'm not as brave as you are. I don't have the courage. Please don't make me go out there!"

The warden could hear Officer Jones's footsteps hustling down the hallway and said, "I'll be right back, Walter. Sit tight for just a minute. I have to speak with Officer Jones now, all right?" Walter wiped the tears off his face and slowly nodded his head.

Officer Jones had recently confirmed the death of Officer Burnes. Once he reached the fifth floor, he rounded the corner and peeked inside cell number 499. He saw Officer Burnes dead in a puddle of blood. The warden walked out of his office, shut the door, and stepped out to the hallway for an update on the search.

Officer Jones said to Dr. Roberts, "Sir, Officer Burnes has been killed in the line of duty. There were no witnesses present, but evidence indicates that McRandle could potentially be the one responsible for his murder."

The doctor said to Officer Jones, "I should have taken McRandle's threats more seriously. I underestimated just how resourceful one lunatic can be in a confined prison. McRandle had a vendetta against Burnes and Nolan after his arrest. There's no doubt in my mind that he's responsible for their murders. Okay, here's the plan, Jones: I want all officers to remain on their normal routine. However, you'll be promoted to acting warden and placed in my office while I'm gone. I'm going to take Walter into the forest with me on the McRandle manhunt."

Officer Jones said to the warden, "That's against our facility regulations. All prisoners must remain inside at all times."

"Fuck regulations!" Dr. Roberts shouted. "I'm in charge, and I'm calling the shots. We're throwing the shackles on the unstable bastard, and I'm taking him out there. I'll have my gun with me if things get dangerous with McRandle. Walter won't be a problem. He's too afraid of his own shadow. We have to make a man out of him sometime, and what better night than Halloween? I'm going in the other room, and I'm going to shackle this pussy up and take him out into the forest. He was a key eyewitness to Officer Nolan's murder, and I need his help with the search. Keep your suggestions concerning the building regulations to yourself, or else I'll withdraw your temporary promotion!"

Officer Jones slowly put his head down in shame and said, "I apologize for my comments concerning the building regulations."

"Save your apologies for later, Jones. All I want from you right now is for you to do your fuckin' job while I'm gone," said Dr. Roberts.

"Yes, sir," said Officer Jones.

The persistent warden walked back into his office and grabbed a pair of shackles from out of his drawer.

The doctor said, "Okay, Walter, I'm going to shackle you up, and we're going to take a journey into the forest to find Herman the clown."

"No, please, I don't want to go out there," Walter said, as he nervously shook in the corner.

Dr. Roberts said, "It's okay, friend. I have my gun, and I'll protect us both. Please help me find the clown."

Walter replied, "I'll go with you to help you find the clown as long as you promise to keep me safe, friend."

The doctor slowly shackled Walter. The doctor awkwardly hesitated for a few seconds, then looked sincerely into McFrancis' eyes and said, "I promise to keep you safe, friend." After Walter was shackled up, the doctor said to him, "Look, Walter, I have a lantern with me. I know that the dark forest makes you nervous, so this will help us see."

Walter twitched a little and replied, "I'm ready to face the forest now. Let's go find the clown."

Dr. Roberts said, "That's the good old Irish spirit, Walter. Let's take a journey into the forest and find the clown."

The warden and Walter exited the private office, where Officer Jones was still waiting. Officer Jones lightly tapped Dr. Roberts on his shoulder and said, "Sir, can I speak with you privately for a brief moment?"

"Sure," replied Dr. Roberts.

Officer Jones and Dr. Roberts walked into the office. Dr. Roberts shut the door and said, "What is it, Officer Jones?"

"Well, one thing I do feel the important need to point out sir, is, have you considered taking an attack dog out there with you on the search instead of McFrancis? I mean after all sir, an attack dog is much more trained for this type of shit than that nervous goofball," said Officer Jones.

"You make a valid point Jones, but I'll have to pass on the idea for now. McFrancis may not be cut out for this type of shit, but he was a key eyewitness to McRandle's breakout, so I'm going to try to use that to my advantage in finding McRandle. I'll have my hands full coddling Walter in the search along the mountainside and I won't be able to bring him and an attack dog along with me."

"I understand, sir," said Officer Jones, even though Dr. Roberts's decisions on the manhunt made no sense to him at all.

"Officer Jones, let me give you a valuable piece of advice on one thing I've learned from my years of experience as a prison warden, 'It's an ugly world out there, so in order to be a successful prison warden you need to throw your fuckin' soul out the window and grow a set of balls.' Remember this, and try to put it to use tonight, okay, pal," said Dr. Roberts.

"Yes, sir. I will Dr. Roberts."

"You're a good man, Jones," said Roberts as he patted him on his shoulder.

"I'll keep things under control around here while you're on the McRandle manhunt," said Officer Jones.

Dr. Roberts said, "I'm sure you will Officer Jones. I have total faith in you. Walter and I will be heading out into the forest soon. When I report back, I'll have you notify Burnes' and Nolan's next of kin. We'll take time to grieve for their deaths after the McRandle manhunt is over. I'll capture that green-haired psychopath, come hell or high water!" said Dr. Roberts as he drew out his handgun and aimed it at the wall. Dr. Roberts left his office. He looked at Walter and saw how nervous he was.

"Come on, Walter. We must head out into the forest now and try to find the clown," said Dr. Roberts. Walter didn't respond. He was too mentally distracted by his nerves to speak at the moment. He just stood there in the hallway and looked at Dr. Roberts as he nodded his head, shaking uncontrollably. He was nervous about the task that lay ahead of him. The warden and McFrancis left the asylum and walked in the direction of the forest, toward where the clown was last seen.

CHAPTER 8

McRandle was already far ahead of Dr. Roberts and McFrancis. Dr. Roberts knew he had wasted some time in calming Walter down and getting him to assist with the McRandle manhunt. The track that Dr. Roberts and Walter were searching for was vacant at the moment, but thirty homicidal maniacs were on the hunt for Mick Patrican, searching the forest not too far from where they were.

During the first five minutes of the search, Dr. Roberts used his lantern to follow McRandle's clown footprints. The exact whereabouts of the clown were a mystery that had Dr. Roberts puzzled. McFrancis was shaking like a little girl the farther they walked into the Dublin Woods.

McRandle was farther down the mountainside and the asylum. Along his travels, he giggled; he thought his escape route was flawless. When he took a few more steps down the mountainside, he walked directly under a giant tree. Once he was under the tree, a mysterious man saw him from under the branches. This man pulled a knife from his pocket as he stalked McRandle. He held his weapon tightly in his right hand. He jumped down on McRandle, blindsiding him and knocking him to the ground.

The mysterious man grunted heavily as he quickly and forcefully decapitated the clown with his knife. Herman's escape route was no longer perfect. The man grabbed the clown's head and put it in his small duffel bag. He searched McRandle and found a handgun in the back of his clown outfit. He noticed it contained no ammunition. The mysterious man pocketed the gun, then vanished from the area unseen. He walked farther down the mountainside and headed to the high-peak riverbed a mile away.

Five minutes later, Dr. Roberts and the nervous Walter approached the giant tree where the clown had been murdered. Walter looked to his left and saw McRandle's body. Walter frantically pointed toward the body and yelled, "Dr. Roberts, I found the clown, and he lost his head!"

The doctor pointed his gun around the crime scene. He walked over and pointed the lantern in the direction of the clown. As Roberts walked a little closer, the frantic Walter started to keel over and cry. Roberts saw the dead clown and that the head was missing. He wondered for a minute what had just happened, and whether someone was stalking him. He looked around and saw no strangers in sight. The doctor searched around the dead body for more evidence—he saw some broken branches, fragments of the clown's torn clothing, and a set of footprints. There was blood on the ground next to the footprints and some of the broken branches. And the clown's torn clothing was soaked with blood. The mysterious man who had killed McRandle had left a trail of footprints on his boots.

Roberts knew that he had a chance to investigate this problem and get to the bottom of it. Three vicious wolves came running in their direction. The wolves could smell McRandle's blood. Dr. Roberts pointed his gun toward the three wolves and shot at them. One of the wolves got shot right between the eyes and instantly dropped to its death. The other two wolves scattered immediately after hearing gunshots. Walter screamed when he heard the wolves howling and three bullets fired. Roberts was a little startled as well. Roberts held his gun in his right hand and his lantern in his left as he walked over to calm Walter again.

Dr. Roberts said, "It's okay, friend. Don't be afraid. My gunshots frightened the wolves and they all scattered. I will protect us."

Walter hugged the doctor. The doctor said to McFrancis, "Now, now, Walter. Let's be men. We need to walk quietly a little farther and see if anyone else is in the forest. Stay close by and tell me if you see anyone."

Dr. Roberts led the way, trying his best to follow the path of the new set of footprints. The two men now walked the Dublin trail in search of a mysterious murderer.

CHAPTER 9

Meanwhile, it had been about an hour since Mick Patrican had murdered O'Neill and O'Connor. The massive manhunt for Mick Patrican was still on as thirty forest-dwelling murderers searched all along the Dublin trails. Patrican had been hiding at the bottom of a hill, and he hadn't moved in a while because one of the guards had been pacing back and forth. The guard flashed his lantern and peeked up the hill.

Patrican slowly and quietly crawled behind a rock to avoid being spotted. The guard looked over in Mick's direction and saw nothing but a rock. The guard decided to walk farther down the trail instead of searching the hill. As Mr. Patrican lay behind the rock unspotted, the guard vanished from his sight. Mick decided to take cover for a few more minutes as the lunatic walked further down the trail.

The next thing Mick saw was a bright green light that came from out of nowhere and glowed right next to him. This glowing green light suddenly appeared to Patrican in the form of a ghost. It was the ghost of General Butch McPherson. The ghost was glowing right in front of Mick's eyes. For a split second, Mick Patrican thought that he was hallucinating. Mick rubbed his hands across his eyes. Then he shook his head. He looked over at this ghost again. He was petrified of this ghost. Mick drew out his small fishing knife and prepared to protect himself. He held his knife out in his right hand. The ghost of General Butch McPherson said, "Patrican. Put your weapon down. I am a friendly ghost who is here to help guide you safely through this dangerous forest. Do not fear me. I am on your side." Patrican took a few deep breaths and put the knife back in his pocket.

Mick said to the ghost, "Who are you? I heard your voice earlier tonight. You were the one who was warning me and my brothers to turn back."

The floating ghost replied, "That's right, Mr. Patrican. I was the voice of friendly warning that you and your brothers should have listened to. I'm sorry that your brothers did not survive the attack. I was General Butch McPherson. I'm showing myself to you because there are certain things that you need to know about this cursed forest. The reason for this is you are a unique person.

"You've survived longer than anyone could've ever imagined possible in the evil forest. Thirty lunatics are on a massive manhunt for you. So far, they've failed to capture you. I have seen the history of these trails for over the last two thousand years. I was the Irish soldier who killed the mummy in the Irish-Egyptian War. The legendary belief of two magical four-leaf clovers was the cause of this war. The mummy that attacked you and mysteriously vanished had one of the clovers implanted inside its heart. A blue alien from a faraway galaxy implanted the clover in the mummy's heart. The clover implanted in the mummy's heart is its greatest strength, but also its greatest weakness. I saw you strike the mummy in its heart. You stunned the mummy when you did this. The mummy has the ability to create havoc in the Dublin Woods on Halloween night because of this evil clover.

"If it possessed the other clover, it would become capable of spreading its evil power all throughout Ireland. I once possessed the other clover, but I lost it deep in a cave during the war. I tried desperately to retrieve the missing, sacred four-leaf clover. Unfortunately, I have been unsuccessful in the search for the missing clover. But the mummy has also been unsuccessful in its search for the missing clover. You must find the missing clover before the clock strikes midnight, defeat this demonic creature, and retrieve the matching clover from its evil heart before it destroys you and all of Ireland. The two magical clovers must be rubbed together and used for good magic, not black magic. That is why you need to find this missing clover before the mummy finds it.

"The Egyptians raided Ireland to try and steal our magical four-leaf clover and use it for evil. The Irish troops outnumbered and outlasted the Egyptians and won the war. There were many casualties on both sides of the battle. I was the last surviving soldier to live on this turf. Therefore, my spirit can live on. The lunatics on these grounds are unaware of my existence. They are permanently blind to this voice and vision as they see and hear only evil. My ability to see into the future is not nearly as clear as my ability to see into the past. You will run into a new threat as you search along this haunted trail for the missing clover. This man is more dangerous than you could ever imagine. He is a murderous fisherman who will try to take you out. The fisherman is an expert at blindside kills, so you must be careful. I can't tell you if you will survive or not; your fate is completely up to you. Now that I have revealed my true self to you, you will never be able to see or hear me again. I must go now and vanish forever. Good luck, Mr. Patrican." The bright green ghost vanished into thin air before Patrican's wide eyes.

Patrican whispered, "Thank you, General McPherson." He felt comforted and overwhelmed at the same time. Patrican continued to lay low for a moment. He had no idea how to find this missing clover. All he knew was that this clover was lost somewhere in a cave. He wasn't up for this dangerous task. But he did understand the importance of it. He just wanted to get out of this cursed forest. He wanted to flee the Dublin Woods, but he did not know the safest way out. Mick decided to make his way up the hill slowly and quietly. After a few minutes, he was about halfway up the top. It was 8:20 p.m., and Mick Patrican had less than four hours to find the missing clover. He was extremely tired. He decided to take a breather and regain some energy.

CHAPTER 10

At the high peak of the trail, there was a small river that the fisherman entered by way of a tiny fishing boat. The fisherman had docked his boat there a short time before he killed the clown. Not much was known about this shady and mysterious man—his real name was unknown to all. His birth mother had dropped his cradle into the sea on October 13, 1850, but he had been rescued by a group of murderous Irish fishermen who taught this child to be evil to the innocent. They had trained him to be a stone-cold killer on land and at sea and to vanish without a trace.

The fisherman had murdered a few people on the Irish seas. The authorities never had leads or witnesses for these mysterious murders at sea. The fisherman had sought this new land to murder by the Dublin River. He had wanted to test his limits with new fishing and hunting opportunities. The fisherman had never served any time in prison or in the insane asylum. He was a rugged man with a scruffy beard who weighed about 225 pounds. The fisherman knew that the Dublin Woods was a dangerous place, but he felt he was the most dangerous new threat the trail had ever faced.

The Irish fisherman lit a victory cigar. "Ah," he said, "that's the sweet taste of a victory kill. The clown put up no fight against me. Fuck the clown! He was a wimp. I decapitated that bastard, then I stole his gun. That's right. I'm the evil fisherman, and I decapitate my victims with my fishing knife. I rule the Dublin River and anywhere that I embark. I have a collection of decapitated heads."

As he grabbed McRandle's head from out of his duffel bag, he laughed and said, "The clown head! My newest trophy!" The fisherman pointed at his duffel bag and said, "I've got two more heads in my duffel bag. I cut off their heads on the Irish seas last month. I've got a few more heads in my boat, but I'm most proud of the clown kill. I fear no one who roams the Dublin trails. How about a second or third kill for me on this epic Halloween night? Come on, who's next?"

The fisherman put McRandle's decapitated skull back into his duffel bag. He took a chug from his whiskey bottle and a drag from his cigar. He finished off his whiskey, stomped out his cigar, and started to gather sticks and rocks to build a small fire pit. Once the fire pit was together, he struck a match and lit the fire. As the fire slowly started to burn and smoke, the fisherman heard a small noise a short distance away.

The man drew out his fishing knife and slowly crept with cautious eyes in the direction of the noise. He held his weapon tightly in his right hand. The bushes started to shake as the fisherman crept toward them—Mick Patrican had now reached the top of the hill. Once Patrican stood up, he and the fisherman looked each other square in the eyes. The distance between the two of them was five feet. The fisherman pointed his knife at Patrican and said, "You're dead!"

Patrican drew out his slightly smaller fishing knife and said, "Fuck you, asshole!" They both charged toward each other, and the battle was on.

The fisherman swung his knife right at Patrican's throat. Mick managed to slide back and duck his body under the fisherman's attack. Patrican swung his knife and cut the fisherman's right hand and wrist. The fisherman immediately dropped his knife in the bushes. This was a brutal wound, and the fisherman groaned in pain, but he kept fighting. He punched Patrican in the face with his left hand. Patrican dropped his knife as he fell on the ground and into the bushes. The fisherman jumped into the bush to attack

Patrican. The two enemies rolled around and wrestled in the bush, looking for the knives.

The fisherman started to strangle Mick with his bloody hand. Patrican started to gasp for air as the fisherman searched the bushes with his left hand for one of the lost knives. Patrican noticed that the fisherman had managed to grab hold of a knife. Just before the fisherman could slice Patrican's throat, Mick drew his left elbow back into the fisherman's sternum. The fisherman had the wind knocked out of him, and he dropped the knife into the bushes again. Patrican turned around and punched the fisherman in the face with a quick right hook. The fisherman dropped into the bushes as Patrican fell on him. They struggled to force each other off the hill near the bush. As they were both trying to throw each other off the hill, they both tried to stay on level ground.

The fisherman out-muscled Mick and got in a position to throw him off the hill. Patrican's feet dangled down the hill as he held tightly onto the fisherman's neck. The fisherman was trying to reach the bush for one of the lost knives. Seconds later, he grabbed hold of a knife. The fisherman swung the blade close to Patrican's throat, but Patrican managed to block the hand with the swinging blade, and the fisherman dropped his knife down the hill.

Patrican punched the fisherman in the face with a quick right jab. Mick was still gripping the fisherman's neck with his left hand. The fisherman shook himself free and drew back into the bushes. As Patrican got up, he put up his two fists and approached the fisherman. The fisherman quickly moved both of his arms around in the bushes in hopes of finding the other knife. The fisherman managed to find Patrican's knife and held it up. The fisherman moved around with the knife while Patrican held up his two fists.

The fisherman was thrusting multiple right-handed knife attacks toward Patrican. Patrican kept shifting around and backing away from these dangerous attacks. These two rugged men were now fighting more toward middle ground. About five feet to their left was a ten-foot drop into a shallow part of the river.

The warden and Walter were traveling a few minutes away and could see a small fire and smoke rising in the dark air. They both walked a little farther, and the warden thought he could hear heavy breathing. The doctor said, "Let's quietly move over this way, Walter. I can see a fire, and I hear voices over in this direction."

Walter drooled and nervously twitched a few times and said, "Okay, Dr. Roberts." They walked quickly in the direction of the fire.

Patrican was still ducking and dodging the fisherman's knife swipes. From the corner of Mick's eye, he saw the clown's head roll out of the duffel bag. The clown's head lay sideways on the ground as his jaw started to move. The evil voodoo spirit of Herman McRandle said to Patrican, "Hey, Patrican, I want revenge on the fisherman! I know you can hear me! The fisherman killed me! I'm dead because of him! You cut off his fuckin' head! If you fail me, I'll make sure your body rots out here forever just like your brothers!"

Patrican tried his best to focus on the fight instead of the terrible voice of the haunting clown. The fisherman also heard the demands of the talking clown. But he remained focused on the fight. The voodoo curse from the afterlife gave McRandle visions of the haunted trail's violent past—his hazel-colored demon eyes could see the brutal executions of Mick's brothers. The doctor appeared from out of nowhere and shot the fisherman in the abdomen. The fisherman groaned in pain as he dropped off the ten-foot ledge and into the shallow riverbed. The fisherman dropped the knife during the fall. Patrican noticed that the doctor was aiming the gun at him now, so he decided to bail down the hill. The doctor shot at Patrican and managed to hit his right hamstring with a silver bullet. When the doctor and Walter moved toward him, Patrican rolled far down the hill and vanished from range. Patrican rolled down the hill a few hundred feet until trees and rocks stopped his momentum. The fisherman groaned in pain from down in the shallow riverbed and shouted, "I'm shot! I need a doctor!"

As Dr. Roberts and Walter stared down at the injured fisherman, the clown's head started to speak to them. The cursed clown said, "Hey, Roberts, it's me, Herman McRandle, the evil clown."

The doctor said, "So the evil curse that you claimed about the afterlife is true after all. The rumors of some of our former patients residing out here in the Dublin Woods also appear to be true."

The clown said, "I got my revenge on Burnes and Nolan, but the fisherman killed me. I want the fisherman's fuckin' head! I'll fuck with you for life unless you give me what I want. Roberts, I want you and that fuckin' pussy to grab the fishing net from the fisherman's boat. Then you use that fuckin' net to drag the fisherman up to level ground, then go a mile due west until you reach the guillotine! Don't you fail me, Dr. Roberts! I want my fuckin' revenge!"

Dr. Roberts knew that he had no choice but to comply with the cursed clown's evil demands. Dr. Roberts noticed that Walter was extremely jittery. "Walter, look at me for one moment, please," said Dr. Roberts. Walter looked at the doctor. The doctor noticed that Walter was breathing nervously, and tears were pouring from his eyes. "Walter, I know that you're frightened by the talking clown head, but I need you to be brave here. Take a few slow deep breaths and let all the air in and out of your body, just like I told you to do right before we headed out into the forest to search for the clown. The clown just told us to head over to the fisherman's boat and grab the fishing net. I'm sure you heard the clown say that as well, and we better do what the clown says before we piss it off even more, so pull yourself together and let's go get the fuckin' fishing net, you nervous goofball," said Dr. Roberts.

"Okay, Dr. Roberts. Let's go get the fishing net, just like the clown says," said Walter in a nervous tone of voice as he stood there, shaking his body uncontrollably in this dark forest.

The boat was docked on a muddy area of a shallow part of the Dublin River. It took Walter and Dr. Roberts a minute to get to the boat as Roberts shone the lantern ahead. When Roberts set the lantern down, he realized that his backup set of six silver bullets had gone missing. The doctor looked in the six-round chamber of his gun and saw that he had only one bullet left. Thomas Roberts knew that he had to make that bullet count. Dr. Roberts looked at Walter and noticed that he was still uncontrollably twitching.

Dr. Roberts said to Walter, "Damn it, Walter, stop twitching. You're acting like a little girl. I need you to be a man and help me with the fishing net. Your incompetence is really starting to piss me off."

McFrancis replied, "I'm sorry, Dr. Roberts. I'm so nervous out here in the forest. I'll try to be brave."

"See that you do. Because right now, you're fucking things up, kid," said Dr. Roberts.

"I'm very sorry, Dr. Roberts," said Walter.

"I'm less concerned with your apologies right now, and more concerned with the simple fact that you need to grow a set of balls, kid," said Dr. Roberts.

"I'll try, sir," said Walter.

Dr. Roberts and the crying Walter grabbed the fishing net and walked along the muddy riverbank, over to the wounded fisherman. With a burning silver bullet buried in his bleeding abdomen, the fisherman knew that he was now defenseless. The doctor looked down at the wounded fisherman and kicked him in the face three times. Between the forceful kicks to the skull and the bullet wound, the fisherman was knocked unconscious. The doctor searched the fisherman. He found a handgun in the fisherman's pocket. He looked at the gun and knew it was stolen from the institution.

The doctor noticed that the gun was out of ammunition. He pocketed the handgun and had a disappointed look on his face as he looked at Walter. "Walter, get your shit together and help me wrap up the fisherman in the damn net!"

"Sorry, Dr. Roberts. I'm so scared right now."

Dr. Roberts shook his head in frustration. He was sick of having this shackled coward trailing along with him in the forest. Walter began to comply with the doctor's requests as nerves and anxiety overwhelmed his senses. They pulled his body up and rolled it into the fishing net, and then they both dragged his body up over the jagged rocks and rough terrain. Within a short time, they reached level ground. Dr. Roberts said, "Thank you for your assistance, Walter. You are no longer necessary."

The doctor cracked the butt of his gun directly on the skull of the shackled mental patient. Walter was dazed, and he lost his balance and fell down the hillside opposite the riverbed. McFrancis started to cry and panic as he rolled down the hill in his shackles. After rolling down the hill a few hundred feet, his body crashed into a thick tree trunk. The tree stopped his momentum, breaking his ribs.

Walter frantically yelled, "No! Doctor Roberts, you said that you were my friend and that you were going to protect me. Doctor Roberts, I need help. Save me, Lerman!" Walter was severely injured, and he had a speech impediment, so he desperately said, "Save me, Lerman," referring to Herman, the haunting clown.

The doctor betrayed Walter because he was annoyed by his whining and sniveling manner. The doctor said, "Why waste my last silver bullet on a fuckin' pussy?" The doctor grabbed the decapitated skull of Herman McRandle and placed it in the fishing net. He looked at his compass and walked due west, dragging the heavy fishing net along with him as he headed down the slope of the mountainside.

Herman was determined to witness the successful decapitation of the fisherman. Herman said to the doctor, "Hurry up and get a move on! This area will be swarming with guards soon because of that whimpering pussy you just gun-bucked."

The doctor ran as he dragged the injured fisherman and Herman's decapitated skull away from the noisy area. They headed due west by the doctor's compass, in the direction of the guillotine.

Walter, still crying loudly, had drawn attention to his exact whereabouts. Two mentally ill guards spotted him and ran in his direction. Walter cried and said, "I need help. Are you here to save me?"

One of the mental guards replied, "No! We're here to kill you!"

Walter kept crying, "No!" The two mental guards dragged him by his shackled feet to the bottom of the hill. His screams suddenly stopped for a second as he attempted to shake his way free, but the shackles and his previous injuries prevented his escape. He was dragged for a few minutes down a secluded path until it ended. All that surrounded this path was a patch of grass and more trees. There was a fire pit burning, and Walter could see the foundation of a shack and a hanging pendulum.

CHAPTER 11

The designer of the pendulum and resident of the small shack was Martin Killington. Martin was responsible for the horrific Halloween massacre of 1842. Martin resided on a more secluded section of the Dublin trails than his twin brother, Matthew. The Killington brothers were infamous. Martin and his brother Matthew were identical twins who shared the same look of evil. Matthew had been born six minutes before Martin. The day these two evil bastards were born was October 31, 1827. One could call them both bastards as their father had abandoned them at birth, and their mother had committed suicide by hanging herself when her husband had left her and their newborn twins behind.

The Killington brothers had been abandoned downtown, just around the corner from Flanagan's Pub. Concerned locals walking the streets of Dublin soon noticed this and came to their aid. The Killington brothers had been taken care of and brought to an orphanage in downtown Dublin, but they developed violent tendencies at a young age due to the neglect of their parents. They lashed out at the six other orphans and bullied them. The other orphans feared the Killington brothers.

The Killington brothers had carried their dark past from birth into their adulthood. Today, they turned sixty-five. They were both gray-haired, with old bones, and they both had a decrepit hunchback. Martin had not seen a trespasser roam in his neck of the woods in a little over two years.

Walter was dragged to the pendulum against his will and strapped down by the two guards as tears poured from his eyes and pain rushed throughout his body. Martin's face lit up with a sick smile. "No! Get away from me!" shouted Walter. The two guards had sadistic smiles on their faces as they heard Walter desperately beg for his life. Walter knew now that he was going to die.

"At ease, gentlemen," Martin said. "Let us take a moment of silence before this Halloween execution." The moment of silence was interrupted by Walter's whimpers. The two guards and Martin were angered by this. Walter kept whimpering as he was placed beneath the pendulum blade. He couldn't stop whimpering. Martin yelled in Walter's face, "How dare you make noise during my requested moment of silence! I'll make you shut the fuck up, you whimpering pussy!"

Martin grabbed a metal rod and walked toward the small fire near his shack. Martin placed the metal rod inside of the blazing fire. After about a minute, the rod became as hot as the fire itself. Martin walked back to the pendulum. Martin Killington placed the scalding hot metal rod directly over Walter's mouth. After Killington pressed the scalding metal rod on his face for nearly ten seconds, Walter's lips and tongue had completely melted. Walter was now desperately fighting for air through his nose. Martin took the burning metal rod off Walter's face as melting flesh started to peel from his mouth. Martin tossed the metal rod to the ground and said, "At ease, gentlemen. Let us take a second attempt at a moment of silence before this Halloween execution."

The night was practically silent except for the small amount of breathing coming from Walter's nose. None of the three men could hear Walter making any more noise, so they prepared to take a second moment of silence. Killington and the two guards remained silent as a moment passed.

Martin shouted to Walter, "Any last words before your execution?" The two men laughed at Killington's sick joke. As the guards got serious again, Martin grabbed a rope and lowered the pendulum a foot. He grabbed a separate rope connected to the pendulum blade. Martin began to move the rope and sway the pendulum blade slowly across Walter's throat. As Killington swung the pendulum blade back and forth, it started to drop slightly. The pendulum hadn't cut him yet, but it would after it dropped another inch. Walter now took his last breath of air along with the last sights and sounds he would ever experience on this earth. The pendulum was now lowered one more inch, and it swiped across poor Walter's throat, finally killing him. Blood instantly splattered all over the pendulum blade.

Martin Killington's night was now complete. It had been a few years since his last execution, and he celebrated with evil pride, knowing that tonight was the fiftieth anniversary of the Halloween massacre of 1842. The two evil men stood there as Killington said, "Ha! What a fuckin' pussy!"

The two mental guards laughed with Killington.

CHAPTER 12

Meanwhile, the doctor dragged the fisherman. The doctor had been walking the unguarded west path and the guillotine lay just ahead. The clown said, "You got to take out the Killington brother with your last silver bullet. Then you need to operate his guillotine to decapitate the fisherman and give me my trophy."

The doctor replied, "I understand the purpose of my mission, Mr. McRandle. It would be an honor to assassinate one of the infamous Killington brothers."

The fisherman slowly regained consciousness and was very dazed and confused. He had a concussion from all the blows that he had received to his skull. The silver bullet burning in his abdomen had cooled down a little. He was still in pain as blood gushed from his abdomen. The bullet was still lodged in his body, wreaking havoc with his internal organs. The fisherman yelled, "No! I'm losing blood! I need a doctor!"

Dr. Roberts pointed his gun at the fisherman and placed his finger against the trigger. He acted as if he were going to shoot the fisherman again. The doctor looked at the fisherman and said, "You have a doctor right here. Now quiet, you piece of shit. Your time is almost up."

The threat of another bullet caused the fisherman to stop talking. The fisherman started to lose the ability to realize what was going on. The guillotine station was a few hundred feet away, and the doctor's arms were becoming tired from the dragging. The clown started to speak again. "Okay, Roberts, ditch the net here and go in for the kill. Once Killington is dead, come back for me, and we'll finish this thing off."

Dr. Roberts complied with the clown's insane demands. There had been no sightings of Mick Patrican. Roberts assumed he was dead. Matthew Killington could not see the doctor as he approached. The doctor crept farther along and noticed that Killington stood clueless by his station. Killington stood there with his arms crossed—he had no idea he was about to be shot. The doctor got on his hands and knees and crawled a little closer to the guillotine. Roberts was still about a hundred feet away. Dr. Roberts stood up and took aim, trusting his shot from a distance. Matthew spotted him from a distance and said, "Dr. Roberts."

Matthew noticed a man in the distance and had a feeling that it was him. The two had seen each other's faces many times before in the Dublin Mental Institution. Before another word was spoken, Dr. Roberts pulled the trigger of his small handgun, and his last silver bullet hit Killington directly in the forehead. The doctor had assassinated one of the infamous Killington brothers. Now there was no one in sight of the guillotine station.

The doctor knew that the shot might draw some attention, so he hurried back to the fishing net. Dr. Roberts knew that some of the guards had diverted their attention a mile away where Walter was screaming and crying. The doctor grabbed the fishing net and dragged it toward the guillotine. The clown smiled from inside the fishing net as he could see the guillotine only feet away. As the fisherman regained consciousness again, he saw the rusty setup of the guillotine and realized this would be the last time he would ever have a head. The clown took a vicious bite out of the fisherman's left arm. The fisherman screamed in agony. "Ah! Get the fuck off me, you stupid clown!" shouted the fisherman as he shook his left arm, trying desperately to get the clown off of him. The clown continued to bite the fisherman for a few more seconds. The fisherman groaned in pain again. The clown stopped biting the fisherman. Then the clown spat out blood and chunks of human flesh. The clown spoke to the fisherman and said, "Fuck you, fisherman! We're at war, asshole!" The clown rolled his head out of the fishing net and realized he would soon have a revenge trophy of his own.

Dr. Roberts pulled the injured fisherman out of the fishing net. The fisherman groaned in pain as he was being pulled out of the fishing net. Dr. Roberts forced the fisherman onto his hands and knees and strapped him into the guillotine. The fisherman shouted his last words. "No! Don't drop the blade on my neck! I'm already injured! I need a fuckin' doctor! No!"

Dr. Roberts dropped the blade of the guillotine, and the fisherman's head fell into a wooden bucket under the guillotine. The clown started to praise the doctor. The clown said, "Nice kill, Roberts! That was fuckin' fantastic! Revenge is mine, fisherman! Now I've got your head as my trophy!"

No more than a second later, Patrican snuck up from behind the shed and snapped Dr. Roberts's neck. Roberts immediately dropped to his death. The clown said, "Patrican, where the fuck did you come from? I thought you were dead!"

Patrician said, "Just tell me the safest way out of these fuckin' woods."

The clown said, "Go back up the steep hill and head to the riverbed. You can take the fisherman's boat to a safe passage. You need to hurry up and stay unseen. There's an angry mob trying to hunt you down, and they're onto your whereabouts. I knew there was something unique about your survival skills. Thanks, Patrican, and good luck with your escape."

Patrican headed back up the steep hill toward the fisherman's boat. It was very difficult for Patrican to run fast because of the bullet wound in his right hamstring. His face was still streaked with mud. His mud-covered face and army clothing had temporarily kept him camouflaged and unspotted by the guards searching for him. He could hear the mob running in the distance, but they now spotted him, so he hustled up the hill, moving his legs as fast as humanly possible.

After a few minutes of hard running, he reached the top of the hill. Patrican ran down to the riverbed and dragged the fisherman's boat into the river. Patrican began to paddle fast as arrows shot from a distance and narrowly missed his skull. A few guards jumped into the river to swim after him. A few of the guards were running uphill with swords drawn. They were a few hundred feet behind their companions. One guard still had a vicious dog with him on the hunt for Mick Patrican. The guard had this dog on a leash and the dog was growling because the dog could smell Mick's blood from some distance away. The dog ran closer toward the smell of Patrican's blood. The dog ran so fast that it lost its footing and fell down the hill. As the guard ran uphill, holding tightly onto the leash, the guard lost his footing and tumbled down the hill. The dog and the guard tumbled down a steep section of this hill and both received multiple injuries as they rolled down this hill full of thorn bushes and jagged rocks. The guard lost his grip on the dog leash. The dog and the guard fell down a three-hundred-foot drop in the forest and landed brutally on level ground, and both died instantly. The Protector of the Dublin Woods ran aggressively toward Patrican from a great distance as he angrily shook his spiked bat and tried to catch up. But the evil guards failed. Patrican managed to row the boat out of the sight of the lunatics pursuing him. As Mick paddled, the river started to get rough and choppy. There was not enough moonlight for Patrican to see ahead properly. Patrican became nervous because he knew he was in danger.

Back at the guillotine, the clown had a sick smile on his face. Herman McRandle's last words before his voodoo curse wore off and his evil spirit permanently died were, "Sorry, Patrican, I forgot to warn you about the waterfall! Happy Halloween! Ha, ha, ha, ha, ha!"

The clown's evil spirit permanently died.

As the river got rougher, Patrican's boat started to tip forward. Patrican hit a fifty-foot waterfall, and the boat capsized. Patrican fell down the waterfall and broke both of his legs on jagged rocks. Mick was held underwater by the force of the waterfall. As he thrashed around, he fought to get air. Patrican managed to swim out of the water, even though he was severely injured, and struggled to crawl out of the river with his bloody hands and legs. On Halloween night, 1892, at 8:45 p.m., Mick Patrican started to vomit blood and water as he lay there injured and stranded on the haunted trail of Dublin, Ireland, barely alive.